Books in

The Human-Hybrid Project

series:

Sunchaser's Gambit

Sunchaser's Gambit

Farley L. Dunn

THREE SKILLET

Published in Fort Worth, Texas

 THREE SKILLET

www.ThreeSkilletPublishing.com

Three Skillet Publishing
PO Box 162194
Fort Worth, Texas 76161

ISBN: 978-1-957173-07-8

Printed in the USA

Sunchaser's Gambit

— Book 8 —

The Human-Hybrid Project

Bay City
Uptown East Side

Bay City
Downtown
Bayside

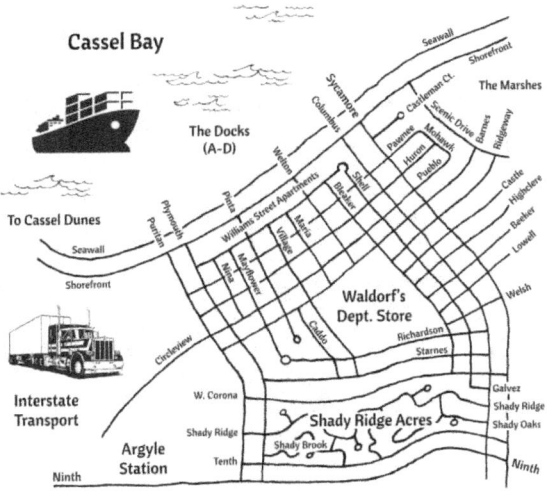

Bay City
Old Town West Side

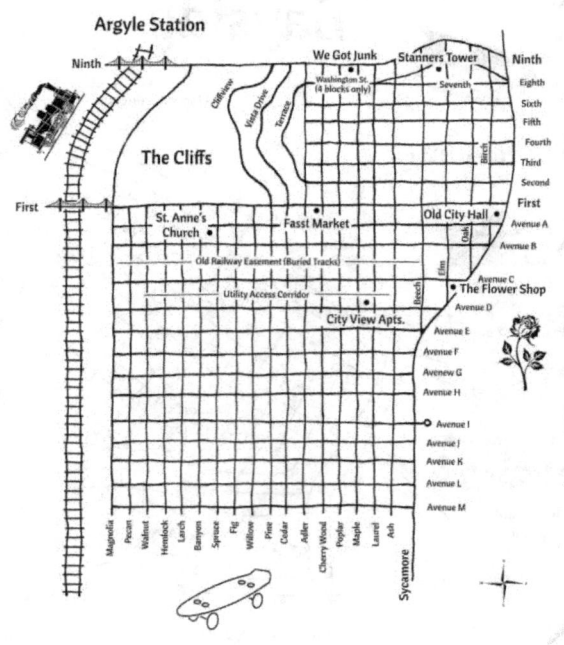

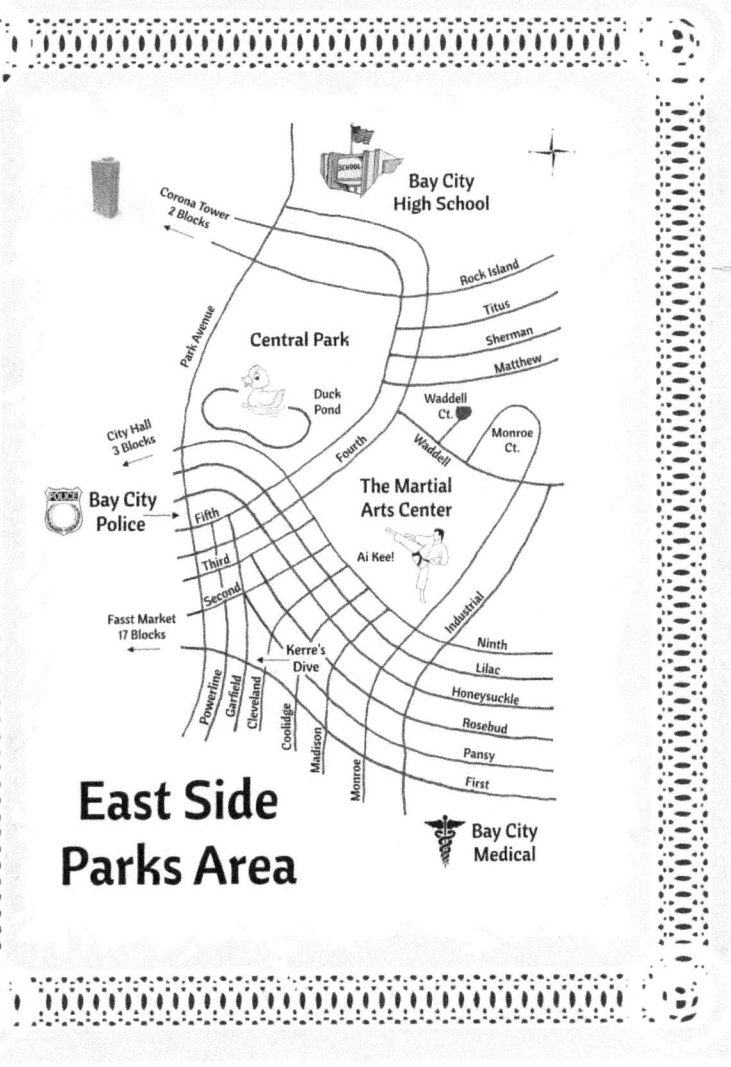

East Side
Parks Area

Bay City
Old Town East Side

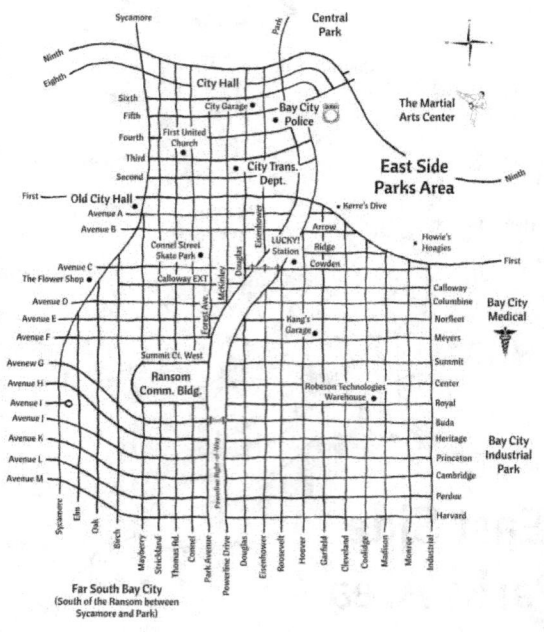

orona Tower scowled from its position on the Bay City skyline, a lone, upthrust pillar of steel and glass, an obsidian blot on a city embroiled in protests, riots, and rebellion.

From Sycamore Avenue, looking north toward The Docks and Harbor Shipyards, the setting sun glinted off the massive monolith into the windows of approaching cars across the city. Garik Shayk, barely eighteen, rode in one of those cars. He had been unwillingly inducted into the Tower's secretive human-hybrid research program. Now part timber wolf and escaped from the Tower's underground warrens and test facilities, he found himself faced with an unbearable decision.

Return to the Tower or risk certain death.

His DNA, irrevocably modified in the Tower's attempts to create the world's perfect super soldier, was glitching, forcing his body into a hyper-enhanced state, short-circuiting his senses and draining energy from him that he could no longer afford to give.

"Hang in there, my friend," Jantzen Hefferly muttered to the nearly unconscious youth. His car dodged through lights daringly, narrowly missing several pedestrians and one car. The urgency was worth the risk. He knew the likelihood of Garik not surviving his ride to the Tower. Jantzen was also modified, although not with something so tame as a wolf. He was half squid, enabling him to sublimate into purple smoke and reform in any location he desired. Purple specks in his eyes were the giveaway, and they increased in number and intensity just before he morphed and disappeared. Jantzen understood the critical nature of Garik's trauma because a man Jantzen had once admired before they became estranged, Weston Rodheimer, had almost been killed by something similar, a glitch in his silverback gorilla DNA modifications. Jantzen had nursed him back to health before becoming part of the project himself.

Now, Weston Rodheimer and his second-in-command, Halo Sunchaser, battled Colonel Brace and his hybrid paramilitary forces for control of the Tower and the military-funded human-hybrid project brewing in the five floors of the building's extensive basement complex. Portions of Bay City had been decimated in the conflict, notably the sections of the city nearest the Tower and along the waterfront. Another sizable area of the city had proclaimed itself a "Tower Free Zone" and now refused access to police, the paramilitary, or anyone who refused to disclaim any affiliation to Corona Tower.

Jantzen was driving into the belly of the beast in an effort to save his teen protégé. Military vehicles sat parked on side streets, with green-suited men patrolling next to black-suited paramilitary hybrids. Remaining on Sycamore, Bay City's main north-south thoroughfare, allowed him to bypass the Tower Free Zone and much of the worst decimation on the east side of town near Central Park and The Martial Arts Center. He slowed at the Corona Street exit, wary of showing his face this close to the Tower. On his own, he could escape anywhere but from a hermetically sealed room, but he had Garik in the car with him. He was locked into his bodily form as long as he controlled this car.

Jantzen weighed his options. He had once been

second-in-command of the research program, the true genius behind the controversial and forward-thinking DNA-enhancement process, but he and Rodheimer no longer shared the same goals . . . and, well, Rodheimer still had all the power, so that told all there was to say about that. Jantzen had run for his own welfare, and in the process, aided the escape of twelve hybrid rejects due for termination. They were his friends, and he refused to let them be parceled out for research or something worse. His betrayal had separated him from Rodheimer, a fracture that couldn't be breached.

"Garik, we're about there. Can you hold on a minute more?" Jantzen glanced at the youth beside him, taking in his curly, dark hair and his strong features. His bronze skin told of his Armenian heritage. His shoulders, now wider than before, and his height . . . Jantzen saw for the first time the growth the boy had undergone since his wolf-based modifications had truly come into their own. No wonder he had been able to perform at a super-human level against Brace's hybridized soldiers. Except Garik wasn't flawed like the men Brace had sent after him. Jantzen didn't consider Garik's current glitch a flaw, more a hiccup that the Tower could address. They had expected it to show up, had hoped it wouldn't, and then when Garik had escaped the Tower . . . well, that's why they were back. In computer terms, Garik needed an update, and Jantzen couldn't provide it without the Tower's mainframe, and to access that meant Jantzen risking his freedom. This was a balancing act he couldn't afford to get wrong. Off one side was the knife edge of death, and the other side was the razor blade of locks and keys, and Rodheimer would not give him any rope this time, not and risk his escape after the trouble he'd caused the Tower.

Jantzen refused to think of what Colonel Brace would do if he got his hands on either of them. They could kiss their tomorrows goodbye.

Garik moaned, his eyes shifted as though he was trying to look around, and he mumbled an unintelligible response.

"What? I didn't catch that." They were nearly to the back of Corona Tower. The area leading to the underground parking garage seethed with suited and armed troops. The hybridized paramilitary men could be identified by the white eagle logo on black dancing on their sleeves. A better indicator was the black full-face helmets with hockey puck-shaped breathing adaptors at their mouths. In a conflict, take them off, and within minutes, they would be wheezing for breath. It was their fatal flaw, the one which Garik was bred to overcome.

"Trap you, too."

"Not if I can help it." Jantzen pulled up to the curb and waited. The youth was the key to the Tower's newest generation of military fighting men who were bigger, stronger, and more resistant to the rigors of war than humanity had ever seen. He must be protected from becoming a research project that might well end in something worse than death.

"Jantz."

"I'm still here." Jantzen could hear the effort in the teen's words. He searched the troops moving about, looking for any sign of recognition. The car he had "borrowed" was nondescript and unfamiliar to anyone searching for them, but that would give them minutes, at best. The Tower had eyes out—and drones over-flying Bay City—and they would find them on a camera somewhere, track them to the burned-out hulk of The Flower Shop, and place them together in this car.

Then they would trace it to right here. Minutes only.

If only he had a watch with him, he could call. Rodheimer would pick up, if only to threaten him, to gloat over his success, even if he had already lost control of the Tower to Brace's forces. It was Garik that Rodheimer wanted, not the Tower, even if the two did go together. He brushed off the hope of a watch. Nothing translated with him when he sublimated from a solid into his purple, gaseous form, so he could carry nothing with him. It was an inconvenience he had learned to accept.

He noticed Garik trying to get his attention. "Yes, say it again, my friend."

"Window." It came out as two whispered puffs of sound, but Garik looked toward the windshield, and

Jantzen understood.

"Window, yes. What about it?"

"Write." Garik tried to raise his hand, but his energy levels were barely keeping him alive. His body was continually attempting to flip him into hyper mode, allowing him to sense, think, and move at speeds almost too fast to be measured. Each time, his "glitch" sent a throb of electric current though his head, but his body couldn't perform. His brain was asking his body to dance, and his body just flopped away, a rag doll instead of a streak of lightning.

"Write. I get it. A note on the windshield." Jantzen began searching for paper and pen. He found an envelope in the glove box and felt under the seat for a pen.

"Lights," Garik tried to say. "Flashers."

Jantzen didn't understand those words, but he and Garik were thinking alike, so he already knew what to do. Write Garik's name on the envelope, stick it in the windshield, and turn on the lights and flashers. Leave a window slightly open, and Jantzen would have plenty of time to vanish as soon as the men were close enough.

He wrote, "Garik Shayk. NEEDS FOOD. Glitching. THE DIRECTOR HAS BEEN NOTIFIED." Well, not yet, but Jantzen would find a phone immediately and let Rodheimer know his precious cargo was alive and waiting below and to get down here before Brace's paramilitary decided to take matters into their own hands once more.

There was an element of danger, for Garik, especially. Hours before, the paramilitary had tried to eliminate him. How many shots had Garik taken? Too many and likely what had triggered his DNA glitch. No one's body, even the best of hybrids, was designed to heal that deeply and that often, and the speed at which Garik had healed had proven to be astonishing.

If the goons decided to move against him before Jantzen could notify Rodheimer, could they kill him? Even the paramilitary hybrids could be destroyed. Likely, the same was true of Garik, just not without effort.

He eased the car to the corner of Corona and McKinley, giving him a view of the residential parking garage that had been bombed by a terrorist and cleared away for access to the underground, highly restricted garage, leaving the entrance now exposed for everyone to see. Men made an anthill of the former garage, going in and out like black insects, knowing their business without anyone seeming to tell them what to do.

His position also allowed them to easily see him.

He pictured the scene he'd left behind when Garik's glitch had forced him from the building. Paul and John down, their bodies broken, lying crumpled on the concrete. The two youths who had tried to help them, neither one hybridized, whom Garik had spirited to safety. Joanie and Justin, well, at least they had gotten out before the fireworks started. If only Garik could have done the same.

"I'm sorry, my friend, that you must go back inside. I have no other options, and I want you to live." Jantzen took the youth's hand, squeezed it, and when he released it, Garik refused to turn loose. Jantzen knew the effort it was taking him, and he squeezed it back. With his other hand, he slipped the note on the dash, words outward, rolled the window partially down, turned on the lights, then hit the flashers. His last thing was to lay his hand on the horn and wait until the men came running.

It took a moment. The horn blared, and one, then two men looked their way. They were slow to react, likely occupied with communications from inside their solid-faced helmets.

"Why aren't they coming?" Garik's words were little more than grunts. He could no longer control his body. All he wanted to do was sleep, to be rid of this feeling, even if in his delirium the electric jolts in his brain calling him to attend had become pleasurable.

"I have to find a phone. I'll help you if I can. I've promised to be your friend, always. I'm not forgetting that just because I'm leaving you now."

Garik could no longer answer, so he forced his energy into his hand. Jantzen squeezed back and evaporated into a purple haze that whipped out the car window and into the darkening evening sky.

Jantzen's clothes sank into the seat. Garik turned his

eyes—he could do nothing else—and saw a fruit bar tumble out of the pocket of the empty shirt.

A fruit bar. He tried to remember the good in a fruit bar. Had Jantzen brought it for him? That was kind of him, though he had no need of a fruit bar. He couldn't eat, could he? He couldn't move. A fruit bar was silly for a person who couldn't chew or eat or think or do anything else.

Garik thought he heard the door open, and he was certain his body fell hard to the side. Hands grabbed him roughly, and a voice called out, "Hey, get Rodrigo. We found the punk, the one we couldn't kill. He's come back for more." Then paper rustled, a short pause, and the same voice said, not as loudly, "That burns my hide."

"What?" Another voice. "What does it say?"

"This one belongs to the Director. He already knows it's here. Target practice has to wait."

"We can still kick it a few times, right?" The second voice laughed.

Garik didn't know the rest. He sank into a rainbow, and it tasted as pretty as it looked.

— 2 —

o one seemed to notice Garik's additional scrapes and bruises as he was bundled on a wheeled gurney and navigated down Stamford Drive and through the entrance to the underground parking garage.

Perhaps they pictured how *normal* he looked after observing the devastation precipitated by his arrival in the garage earlier that day. The remains of weapons fire still scarred the concrete, and bloodstains were just being scrubbed away, so a little physical "damage" could be expected on the youth that had been at the center of it all.

Once he got food, his body would heal the injuries inflicted by the paramilitary goons who had retrieved him from the car, but for now, nurses and medical technicians struggled to keep him breathing and his heart pumping. The short-circuiting rainbows in his head? Good luck with that. He needed a full DNA patch. A software upgrade . . . and a reboot in the process.

A limousine with deeply tinted windows pulled down the ramp into the basement parking garage and stopped alongside the team surrounding Garik. The car flashed its lights and honked to get their attention. The driver's door opened, but the back door flung itself wide before the driver could exit the car. Weston Rodheimer emerged, his massive shoulders dominating every other person, including the oversized and intimidating paramilitary goons.

"This is the boy?" Rodheimer's tone said he expected it to be.

"We think so, sir." A male nurse holding a bag of plasma over Garik's arm lifted one of the youth's eyelids. The pupil contracted, but there was little else to indicate he was alive. "We need to get him downstairs."

"You've seen the video feeds?" Rodheimer raked his eyes up and down Garik. "He doesn't seem that . . . different. Where are the changes, the improvements?

For him to do the damage he did, move the way he did . . ."

"We are looking into that, sir." The nurse was respectful, but he looked to the elevator door. One of his team was holding it open and waiting.

"I want updates. Anything you find. If he comes to, notify me."

"Yessir."

Rodheimer took another long look at Garik, turned, dropped into his car. His driver closed his door after him, climbed in, and the big automobile moved toward the exit, picking up speed until it started the turn up the ramp to the surface.

COME TO? Garik wanted to laugh, but his body wouldn't respond. He was awake, fully conscious, perhaps too much so. In between the searing jolts of rainbow electricity that sliced through his brain, leaving him woozy and perhaps a bit drunk with endorphins, his senses were soaking in the world around him, the sounds and odors and temperature fluctuations. His awareness was flooded with each person attending him, their heartbeats, their breathing patterns, even the scent on their skins. One had a heart murmur, another suffered with asthma, and the cat lady carried the aroma of newborn kittens about her. Too much information, more than he wanted to know.

When they had pierced his arm with the needle to

allow the bag of plasma—oh, so cold!—to flow into him, it had been an ice knife, the sword of an ancient being, a viper's tooth slipping inside to inject him with mind-bending venom and reveal the workings of the world before time and of time to come.

Video feeds, video feeds . . . Garik's brain glitched in rainbow swirls, and he saw what the cameras must have seen. Him, there and gone, flashing in and flashing out. He smiled at the idea of Jantzen flashing in and flashing out, flashing more than he ought. Well, he thought he smiled, but he couldn't be certain.

"The plasma is helping. His facial expression just changed."

Expression, suppression, recession, digression. Mine, yours, hers, theirs? The words flowed around Garik. He heard the ding of the elevator doors—the sound of a cash register, the one-minute bell indicating time to get to class, his watch notifying him he had a message. Hello, Marisa, yes, I can hold your hand, sit under a blanket with you on the roof of our building and watch the stars . . .

His eyes burned. Watch the stars . . . they were all in the sky, and he was riding an elevator into the depths of—an alarm sounded, something outside Garik's head, sharp and insistent. He wanted to push it away. He was sleepy and ready to close his eyes and dream his world the way he wanted it to be.

"Cardiac arrest," the male nurse called, his words

even but his voice tense with urgency. The gurney jumped and leaned as if they were running. He seemed out of breath.

"O.R. 3 is ready, Sean."

The gurney turned sharply and came to an abrupt stop. Garik felt hands on his body, he was lifted, abruptly released. He heard a buzzing sound, felt his head tingle, sensed something on his scalp.

"Brain scans indicate he's still conscious."

"During cardiac arrest?" Disbelief.

This time, Garik's chest grew cold. Someone called, "Clear!" Then, lightning jumped into him, his world went white, and he knew what the buzzing sound was.

They had cut his hair, *again!*

GARIK OPENED his eyes, took a deep breath, remembered Sean's name, smell, and the asthma the man battled; and he absorbed the white ceiling overhead. A light burned in the center.

"Awake." The word rumbled rather than flowed.

"Director," Garik acknowledged. He moved his eyes and found the man at his side. He shifted his gaze and was interrupted before he could scan the rest of the room.

"Brace isn't here." Brace was Colonel Brace, the Air Force brass who had wrested control of Corona Tower from Rodheimer by use of DNA-enhanced super soldiers, albeit soldiers with a respiratory flaw requiring them to supplement their bodily requirements for air with breathing masks. They were unable to absorb enough oxygen from the air to fuel their bodies' inefficient furnaces.

Garik hadn't known all that before, but he saw it now. How? Notice. Quantify. Deduce. It had to be, simply because it *was*.

"Where is—" Where is Nurse Ratchett, Garik intended to ask, but Rodheimer cut off the question with an answer.

"Nurse Fortinier is also not here. It is just the two of us. I've asked for some time alone with you."

Alone? Garik was about to ask why when the big man started talking.

"Why, you are about to inquire. There are things that need to be said just between us. And for your next question, how do I know what you're about to ask so accurately? We are too much alike for me not to understand your thoughts."

Understand my thoughts. Garik kept his face clear of emotion, but the man didn't understand his thoughts at all, or he would understand how much Garik wanted to be free from this place, and he would let him go . . . well, as soon as he fixed the glitching rainbows in his head, but let him go, nonetheless.

"You won't want to leave when you realize what we can offer you, my young friend."

Garik shifted his shoulders, felt his head rub on the

pillow, anger flared, and without thinking, he spat, "What's with the hair-cutting thing? Are you all idiots?"

"Perhaps." Rodheimer smiled. "This time, however, you did it to yourself."

"Blame me. Yeah, that's right." Garik started to sit up, and his arm was affixed to the bedrail. A tube trailed overhead. "What's this?"

"That. Yes. I know you were with Jantzen. I've seen the videos. He must have informed you what you've been going through." Rodheimer ran a hand over one of the readouts for Garik's medical devices. "The numbers these machines are returning, they are unbelievable. I now regret not monitoring your development more closely. I assumed—" He shrugged and turned his attention back to Garik. "I want you to be happy here. It would be best for all of us."

"For you, you mean." Garik could smell the man's anticipation. He wanted this badly.

"Yes, for me. Equally for you. I realize now I didn't allow enough time for your, shall we say, enhancements to come to fruition. You've interacted with Brace's private army." He said *private army* with disdain.

"You don't approve."

"Oh, no, the product we provided is outstanding, mostly. Just incomplete. Brace insisted we give him *something*, but we weren't ready. The man doesn't understand how science works."

"How does it work?"

"Inquisitive. That's good. Your mind is working. That's something Brace's men don't have, the ability to think beyond the current situation. It's something we hope to see in you."

"In me." Garik cringed, and he waited on the man to say, *Repeating others, still?*

"I expected you would see this already." Rodheimer raised an eyebrow. "You are the completion to what Brace's men are missing. The next step. The final evolution, we hope."

"And I'm also broken." With his good hand, Garik indicated the hospital room.

"Not broken. Far from it, my boy. This is an expected bump in the road, one we are smoothing out as we speak." He touched a bag hanging above Garik. "The final ingredient. In a short time, we can begin evaluating how far you've come."

"Where I've come is back to where I started," Garik said bitterly.

"To where you started." Rodheimer looked around the room and chuckled. "Your memory is as good as I'm led to believe. I do think this is the same room where we first met. Halo will be surprised to hear about this." His chuckle became a laugh, and he turned, Garik already dismissed, opened the door and stepped outside, leaving the door ajar. "Dr. Jamie, I am finished. Testing perhaps tomorrow?"

"If you wish, Director. An extra day would be better for accurate results."

"If we must. I will expect him fully fixed and that defect in his head gone. If only Jantzen were here. This was his specialty. That's old water, though. Can't be helped, and I'm sure you have Jantzen's records for reference."

"Yes, Director. No mistakes this time."

"Make sure. I don't want to lose this one, too."

LOSE THIS one, too. How many had they lost? The names flashed through Garik's head: Christian, Paolo, Alyna, Joanie, Giselle, Amy, Leigh, Laura, Paul, John, Justin, Marco, and now, Jantzen.

Jantzen was at least alive. Garik couldn't be sure about the rest. He'd seen Paul and John on the floor of the garage, their clothing painted red. Christian, sent away somewhere for research, either whole or in parts.

Nurse Fortinier came in, interrupting his thoughts, and she held a vial and a needle.

"Not the needle." Garik groaned. "I'm awake. I'm fine. I'm not fighting or argumentative. I'm being good."

"You need to heal," she said. "This will help."

"Help put me to sleep?" He remembered the sleepy juice. He'd slept most of the first few weeks here.

"That too. And I'm sorry about your hair. It's a shame it had to be cut again. It was growing out beautifully." She took his good arm and rubbed it with an alcohol swab. She pressed the needle against his skin, it slipped inside, and the cool liquid surged through him.

It was different this time, though. The rainbows in his head, lessened but not gone, might have been the difference, or maybe it was that he was becoming something other than even the Tower's research teams imagined. The drug flowed in, a poison of sorts, though not one that would kill him. He sensed the compounds as they moved into his blood. He felt their composition, the arrangement of the molecules, and he instructed his white blood cells to shift an enzyme, relocate a peptide, and in the doing, change the structure of the poison, mitigating the toxicity of the drug.

He didn't negate it. He turned it into a soporific, something to make the time flow faster, to put his mind in another place, to have back what had been taken from him, if only for a short time.

He closed his eyes and dreamed of Marisa, the way their life should have been.

"That's it. Sleep away." Nurse Fortinier withdrew the needle and exited, leaving Garik alone with his dreams.

— 3 —

ow tall did you say?" Sheesh, Garik thought. Even their machines didn't work down here. No wonder this place had messed up so many of their "super soldier" hybrids.

They couldn't even measure how tall he was!

"Five-eleven. Is that surprising to you?"

"Yes. That can't be right." Five-eight, always and forever. He could prove it. It was on his license. A momentary surge of anger hit him before he choked it off. Right! They had taken that from him, too. Sheesh!

"I can double check." Sean Ito, the nurse who had wheeled him in—and smelled of asthma—stepped away and tapped numbers into a tablet sitting on a counter.

"Please." He had stopped growing when he was fifteen. People didn't just shoot up three inches when they turned eighteen. No one got that as a birthday bonus. Yet, in the elevator with Airman Vang. And Dieter's comment, *"You are taller . . ."*

"Let's use the laser scanner this time." Sean didn't seem put off that Garik doubted his skills, just opened an adjoining door and waited for him to step through.

As he moved past, Garik did notice he was eye to eye with the man, a little over, if anything.

"And you are?" He glanced about, noting the array of high-tech devices, unlike the manual height and weight machine he had been on for his INACCURATE HEIGHT MEASUREMENT.

"Sean Ito. You likely don't remember—"

"I know your name," Garik barked, before he caught himself. Sean had not been unkind, the opposite, in fact. He knew what it was. His anger at being here was bleeding out, affecting how he saw things. Also, they had pumped him full of fresh DNA sauce, and while it might need to marinate in his veins a while, he was ready to come out of the oven. He now saw the world in permanent rainbow shadows, calling to him, whispering, faster, faster, *faster*, *FASTER*. The repeated jolts of electricity feeding into his brain, stoking his endorphins, were a metronome, an addictive reminder that he was different, changed, and likely deadly to himself if he let the rainbows take control. His brain now bled rainbows, deadly arches that fed on who he was, wanted to suck him dry in exchange for a feeling of endorphin-charged power . . . and speed . . . and forgetting what had been done to him without his permission . . . and could never be undone—

"Garik? Are you with me?"

He shook his head to force the rainbows into the background and let the white, antiseptic room expand to fill his vision. How many times had Marisa said that to him to bring him back from la-la land?

"I'm sorry, Sean. I was—" What? Dreaming of deadly rainbows? He couldn't say that, and he was embarrassed that he had snapped at the man. He tried again. "It was inconsiderate of me to cut you off. Do you mind telling me your height?"

"Not at all and thank you for the apology. Not too many of those come my way down here. Five-nine. Why?" He indicated a square marked on the floor inside a glass-walled structure.

"I was eye level when I walked by you."

"Bit above. I'm pretty good at judging height." He shrugged and grinned. "Practice. I do this frequently. My machine says five-eleven for you. I could judge that even before you got on the scale. This one also gives your shoe size."

"I need that?"

"If you've grown, your feet will have, too. New shoes for you!" Sean stepped to the side of the unit. "Hands to your side. We'll know every inch of you after this. Remain perfectly still. Don't want you to come out with four arms."

"It can do that?" Garik had seen weirder. He didn't want it to be him.

"Only on the results. You want four real arms, you've got to grow them yourself. You might close your eyes. The laser can surprise you."

The lasers flashed, Garik fought his rainbows, and he imagined himself as he used to be. Average size, lean and tight from riding skateboards, with a thick mop of curls he could tie in a bun. Now, he was tall and bald. Well, tightly buzzed. Not a fair exchange, not one he would have made in a million years.

"Done," Sean called. "Come on out."

"It says?"

"What I said, five-eleven, maybe a smidge over. Shoe size eleven—"

"Can't be right." Garik studied the readout. It showed his image in full color, bald head to shoeless feet, with measurements. "That's me?"

"I wasn't in there. Let me print this. It saves to your file automatically, but I can give you a copy."

Garik heard him, but he was focused on the image on the screen. Shoulders, thighs, forearms. It was his face, but the rest of him was not what he remembered from his mirror. Had his hours in the pool, games on the racquetball courts, time on the climbing wall done this? He didn't feel that different, well, except things were easier—running, climbing, laps in the pool—so there was that. Maybe . . . it was too much to think about, too many changes in his life, and he turned when Sean cleared his throat.

"Now, we have some tests to run. The Director has asked to attend, so shipshape! Show him what your ticker can do. He seems to have high hopes for you." Very upbeat and encouraging.

Sean led him out the door, pointed to his shoes, and casually remarked that he'd noticed how quickly he'd healed since wheeling him in from on the street where they'd found him. That puzzled Garik. He'd been with Jantzen in the car, not on the street. Then he remembered the goons, *"We can still kick it a few times, right?"* and the rainbows threatened to take control, pulsing in his head with electrical jolts of precision pain.

He chanted to himself, "Anger gets me nothing. I must use my hands, my mind, my desire to achieve what I want."

"A question?" Sean smiled pleasantly.

"Practicing self-control. Hoping it works."

"Mr. Rodheimer will be pleased, I'm certain."

Garik breathed deeply and let the rainbows fade, becoming a background surge of finger-in-the-socket reminders that they weren't gone. They didn't go away. They never did any longer.

He wondered what the tests would be this time. Sixteen bricks and a bag of sand? Likely. They seemed to expect more of him every time he was tested.

The reality that he could only blame himself was a black cloud. He had Houdinied out of this place twice, and he was back again. Sheesh! He wanted to hit himself in the head. He felt as stupid as they were!

He firmed up his resolve. Where a man can Houdini once, he can Houdini a second time. *Get these rainbows out of my head, and I'll be gone all over again.*

Bet on it, Mr. Rodheimer. And you can take that to the bank.

AT A SIGNAL, Garik slowed his stationary bike and dropped his forehead to the handlebars. Sweat streamed from him. He was down to shorts, a monitor was strapped to his arms, sticky pads were wired all over his torso, and he breathed into a tube wedged into his mouth.

"Let me take this." Loren Gershon, with red hair and freckles, reached under him and placed her hand around the breathing tube.

Garik raised his head and allowed her to slip it upward as she released the straps around his scalp. One check mark for a good buzz cut, he thought. Nothing to get tangled in the straps. The sticky pads on his body? They had removed all the hair there, too.

Remembering that, he thought, what next? Armpits? Do you really want to go there? Just try it!

Through a glass wall in front of him, in an adjacent observation room, Director Rodheimer lifted a handset wired into the arm of his chair. He was surrounded by a cadre of associates. Halo Sunchaser was missing, and of course, there was no sign of Colonel Brace. He was likely off laying claim to what was left of Bay City, along with all military personnel not currently guarding the entrances and exits to the basement research center.

"Dr. Jamie, well?"

"Yes, Director, I have the results you wish." The man kept his eyes on his monitor as he spoke, his gaze flicking from point to point, indicating he didn't quite "have" it. Then he smiled and relaxed. A printer next to him whirred, and he lifted the printout and stood.

"Well?" Rodheimer's voice, so low the speakers had trouble conveying its timbre precisely, resonated in the room. He still held his handset to his ear.

"Amazing, Director, simply amazing. The readouts—" he held out the paper towards the window with one hand and tapped it with the other, "—are approaching the parameters of Colonel Brace's people, and there are no signs of oxygen deprivation when the body is under full stress."

"So, lung capacity—"

"Never a problem, even with Brace's people. It's the absorption rate, the ability to metabolize the oxygen that's the issue there. Garik, well, his chest size says it all. The numbers show lung capacity more than fifty percent above standard, which means his heart . . ." Jimenez grinned, studied the printout as though he couldn't believe his good fortune, and drew in a deep, satisfied breath.

"And, Dr. Jamie?"

"Right, right." Jimenez looked toward the window, his eyes bright. "All top athletes, as you surely know, develop enlarged hearts—"

"Enlarged?" Rodheimer frowned. "A disease? Cardio . . . ography? That's not a good thing, doctor."

"No, this isn't cardiomegaly. The muscle walls are not thickened or in any way injured." He laid the paper aside. "An athlete's heart stretches to pump more blood —enlarging the ventricle and thereby allowing a lower resting heart rate. That's a very good thing. Here's what's important. More blood means more oxygen, which means faster muscle response, greater endurance, and a quicker recovery rate."

"And the, um, issue we are attempting to resolve?"

Not *issue*. Brain glitch, Garik thought, wishing people would quit sidestepping the issue. Just say it. We all know it happened . . . was still happening, even if it was better than before. And he was living with it. Who did they think they were hiding it from?

"The treatment seems to have been successful."

Treatment. Garik reminded himself he was in control of his emotions. His hands, his mind, his desire. It was no treatment. They had given him an upgraded DNA infusion. Now he was likely to grow claws and a tail, and he would for sure howl at the next full moon.

Rodheimer seemed to be evaluating Dr. Jimenez's answer, his eyes on Garik, seeing the newly shorn head, the broader shoulders, the extra height on his frame. Then he relaxed slightly, shifted his arms, tilted his head differently, and his face lost its intensity.

"Good news, then, Dr. Jamie. A shower and fresh clothes, then I want to meet with both of you." Rodheimer replaced the handset, carefully for a man of his immense bulk, stood, and made his way out of the observation room. The rest of his cohorts followed him one at a time.

"MR. SHAYK, Garik, come in."

Director Rodheimer personally held the door. His offices in the research center lacked the views from his penthouse suite at the top of Corona Tower, but it was as luxurious in every other way.

"Dr. Jamie, please." The Director invited Jimenez to join them, and he showed them to a group of Le Corbusier chairs in blocky black leather and chrome.

From a small refrigerator hidden inside a wall of cabinets, he withdrew three bottles of chilled water, offered one each to Garik and Jimenez and kept the third for himself. He sat and placed his water on a glass table at his side.

"How has your stay with us been, Garik? Have you been well treated?" The Director smiled and seemed truly interested.

Garik looked to the doctor and back to the Director, unsure what game they were playing. He decided to go along and said, "So far, except for the tests—"

"Over." Rodheimer laughed. "Hear that, Dr. Jamie? No more tests for our young friend. There are no reasons for more tests, are there?"

"Um, no, I suppose not, although there are endurance parameters I would like to probe—"

"That's that, then. Garik, we have new quarters for you. How would you like a room with a view? Penthouse level, will that do? Here's your new passkey." He slipped one from inside a pocket and tossed it hard Garik's direction.

Garik caught it, the rainbows swirling, and immediately let them slip away, in control once more.

"That's what I thought," Rodheimer said, smiling. "Good as new."

Penthouse, but with a catch. Garik wondered the price Rodheimer would expect him to pay.

— 4 —

hat is this?" Halo Sunchaser in a bright pink and jet headwrap appeared in the room. Her hawk-like eyes peered from her ebony face, made more menacing by the round silver earrings that dangled at her jawline.

She took in each member of the cabal: Weston Rodheimer, casually at ease, his expression revealing how pleased he was; Garik, the new passkey held aloft, studying it, attempting to weigh out its value in favors and compromises; Dr. Jimenez as the odd man out, neither friend nor foe, neither Tower royalty nor basement rabble.

"A meeting, Halo." Rodheimer smiled, equal to equal, giving her that. Then he took it away. "You do understand meetings, where deals are worked out, alliances formed, relationships that breed success. It's how a successful business moves forward."

"Business." She dropped her wrap in a vacant chair, exposing a pink paisley suit in a business cut, with black and pink suede flats. She walked along the back of Jimenez's chair. He turned his head to follow her as best he could. "Doctor business, I presume. Checkups, weight regimens, perhaps even the correct *medications* to keep our new subject from escaping once again and embarrassing us all over."

"He is the doctor," Rodheimer remarked, dryly. "That *is* what the good doctor does."

"Then there's this one." She was to Garik, and she took a finger and ran it along his jawline. "What does the good boy do?"

Garik kept silent. He had seen Sunchaser's electrified sword at work, watched it eat a fellow hybrid, dissolving her until there was nothing left but empty space, not even a pile of ash to collect and mourn. The doctor would be quaking in his chair if he had seen what Garik had seen. Then, he supposed it best he hadn't. The bedlam in the parking garage that had left

John and Paul crumpled on the floor was nothing in comparison.

"And this." Sunchaser gently lifted the passkey from Garik's palm and balanced it in her own. "A passkey, and in the boy's hand."

"Not much of a boy any longer, Halo. Look at him." Rodheimer came very close to a smirk before letting it fade from his face. "Third generation and very near flaw-free. For the second time he has returned to us, of his own accord."

Returned to them, yes, but of his own accord? The first time he saw how Rodheimer might have thought that, and Garik hadn't corrected him. This time, however, he had battled for his freedom and only returned when he accepted that his life was forfeit without the Tower's help. Sheesh! Next, they would be saying he was the savior of the Tower's plans to usurp Brace's newfound and irritating domination of the Tower's operational sector.

"Has he, Weston? I wonder." She sat elegantly on the arm of Garik's Le Corbusier, placed one hand on his scalp, and gently stroked the stubble that was just starting to regrow. "We have been breeding for independent thinking, the ability to outmaneuver an opponent mentally. When we get it, it comes with intractability, the refusal of our subjects to adhere to our plans. If we get cooperation from our subjects, they are no more than mindless machines, such as Brace's men.

A pity. They fight so well not to have a thought in their heads. Then there's this one, very near flaw-free, allowing him to think and do all those things we saw on the video feeds. Hmm."

"Get to the point, Halo. I assume there is one." Rodheimer, his tone even, his expression ready to move on.

"Someone once swapped my passkey." She held up Garik's and studied it. "Then, this *boy* allowed himself to be trapped and inserted into our program—"

"Halo." Rodheimer's word held a warning.

"Allowed, Weston. And we didn't see it. He is out-manipulating both of us. He returned, and another of our participants is gone. Now, Paul, one of our best creations, and John, whom I'm sure would have been outstanding, if we could have harnessed his skill, are lost. I'm sure of it. We've DNA matched the blood. I'm told they couldn't have survived."

DNA matched the blood . . . couldn't have survived . . . that meant they also didn't have the bodies. Could there be a chance for Paul and John? All hybrids were hardy, and they healed quickly. A small amount of hope welled up in Garik.

The other things Sunchaser was saying were way off the mark. He had nothing to do with stealing her passkey. That was all Marisa's fault. And returning? What did that have to do with additional hybrids escaping? The first time he returned, they captured him with video feeds and a BolaWrap, both of which were unfair and not part of any plan he had concocted. Just the opposite. The second time? It was their fault he was back, their flaw in him, and he harbored no plan, no intent, and no desire to stay, thank you. Give me my receipt, show me the door, and I'm outta here. Next she would be saying he had caused the whole Rodheimer-Brace debacle, plunging Bay City into a cauldron of riots and terrorist incidences.

"Halo, can we discuss this in private?"

"Certainly. Dr. Jamie, do you mind?"

Jimenez looked at Rodheimer, and when the man nodded, he stood. He motioned to Garik, but when Garik started to stand, Sunchaser touched his shoulder firmly to indicate he wasn't to leave.

"Go, Dr. Jamie. It's okay." When the man exited, Rodheimer asked, "Halo, the empty chair, please? The doctor didn't touch his water. Feel free."

"This," she said, holding out the key. "A penthouse key. What are you thinking, Weston? He's already escaped twice, right under our nose. What makes you think he won't walk out the front door the moment we're not looking?"

"The apartment and the Stamford Suites amenities. That's all it accesses."

"And the research facility?"

"Just the apartment and the amenities available to Stamford Suites. And before you tell me every other way he could exit, you are right on each one, except that I have covered those, too."

She stood, dropped the key into Garik's hand, and moved to the empty chair. She selected the bottle of water from the table, twisted the lid loose, and took a sip. When finished, she said, "Elaborate."

Rodheimer spoke to Garik. "I would have explained later, but now's as good a time as any since my hand is forced." He cut his eyes to Sunchaser before looking back to Garik. "We've installed a tracker. You can remove it, but it will be difficult. I don't suggest you try. You might do, um, other damage you might not find acceptable. It will set off an alarm if you are out of bounds for more than ten minutes."

Garik studied the passkey. This was his price. The gleaming device didn't hold the same appeal. He looked up, a quick glance at Sunchaser to see a smug smile and a longer look at Rodheimer.

"The apartment, the pool, and the gym." He had lost everything once again. He might as well push to see what he could gain. "The restaurant? I might get hungry now and again."

"You will have room service, but I'll see about adding the restaurant to your permissions."

"The hospital, the mall, or have I lost all that?"

"Let me think about it—"

"Weston," Sunchaser snapped, "don't let your hopes cloud your judgment. This boy has already removed your number two man from your employ.

Jantzen would still be in the research labs . . ."

She kept talking, but Garik's head was white with confusion. Did she think he held any power at all in this place? Jantzen had organized and aided every move of his first escape. The next one had been Paul's doing, none of his.

Garik was yanked back into the conversation when Rodheimer barked, "Enough, Halo. Leave my wife out of this. I am not looking for a replacement for my unborn son. How dare you say that. The number two spot in this organization remains unfilled as a memorial to my and Jantzen's old friendship, and it will continue to remain so. I will be the one to decide if someone will someday move into that slot."

The air was tense. In the silence, Garik picked up on Rodheimer's heartbeat. Slow, steady, not missing a tick. Sunchaser's was fiery hot with anger and indignation. This was more than an argument over the position Jantzen had vacated when he left the Tower. Sunchaser felt the rebuff was personal, as if Jantzen leaving the program affected her on a more intimate level than it should. Her accusations sounded closer to retribution than reason.

Once more, he wondered what game Jantzen was playing and who all was involved. Before he could spend any time working it out, Sunchaser was gathering her things and on her way out the door.

"MY APOLOGIES," Rodheimer said, taking a long swig from his water bottle. "You should have been allowed to leave. I meant the key to be a symbol of my trust in you, not of the restrictions you must endure. You must understand, Halo is right about some of what she says, although less diplomatic than I might prefer. The key will allow you a great deal of freedom—"

"And I have been chipped and validated. If I'm lost or wander off . . ." He stared at the bigger man.

"What I understand and not everyone does is the need for independent thinking, for a soldier to find himself in a hostile situation, evaluate the information he is given, and decide on a plan of action. Good soldiers can infiltrate the enemy, pose as one of them, and still get their job done, even return to base to receive a new assignment. You've appeared to master that. My question to you: Are you a good soldier?"

Garik considered the question. He was with the enemy. Could he evaluate the information he was receiving and decide on a plan of action that would allow him to HOUDINI OUT OF HERE?

"Absolutely. Always." He made sure his voice was utterly sincere.

"I saw that in you. People want to join us, but few manage to infiltrate us the way you did. I knew I wanted you on this team the night of your intrusion. It takes guts to embark on such a plan. I was disappointed to lose Jantzen, but he and I were headed opposite directions. He and I were quite close once. Did he tell you that?"

Garik nodded. He'd told him much more than that, even though Garik suspected it hadn't all been intended for his ears.

"Childhood friends. He was the one there for me when I suffered what you've just gone through. Jantzen came up with the cure, if we want to call it that. He never did, but I like the way it sounds. A cure for what ails us, meaning those of us who have been upgraded."

"What does Jantzen call it?"

"Oh, Jantz?" Rodheimer chuckled, using the nickname unexpectedly. "Jantz likes to say we were rebooting the system. I never liked to think of myself as a machine. Cure. That's much better. How does it feel to be cured?"

The colors in the room glitched, Garik controlled it, and the addictive buzz reverberated in his skull, painful in a very pleasurable way.

"It feels good, Director."

"Fine. Let's show you your room."

ROOM? ROOMS. A whole suite of rooms.

A tiny kitchen—at least they didn't expect him to cook—with a dining room, an office, a living room, and a loft. Two bedrooms completed the suite, each with a private bath. The walls, broad expanses of glass with views south and west over the city. Northwest he could just catch glimpses of The Docks and Cassel Dunes along the shore.

The closet revealed the extent of the Tower's involvement in the lives of its citizens. Racks of clothes sized to fit his new shoulders, and shoes. Who could wear so many, and all in his new size eleven? He shook out a pair of pants, held them to his waist, and was pleased to see that they landed just at the tops of his shoes—which he hadn't noticed were too tight for him until he was measured by Sean. He kicked them off and knew he would never wear them again.

One thing he was determined to find: pajamas. In these places, people tended to come in and out like he had a revolving door. If he was sleeping in one of these beds, he wanted to be presentable all hours of the day and night.

Looking out over the city was when he became heartsick. Halfway up Stanwick Hill, Sycamore jogged west, exposing the blackened remains of The Flower Shop. Three blocks west, the rooftop of City View Apartments. The view would be gone in the summer, but now, it was a connection with Marisa.

Then the doorbell chimed, and someone called, "Room service."

Garik was hungry, and he moved away from the window to answer the door.

— 5 —

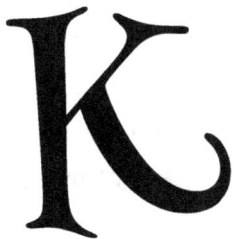

ofi Mandela, the twenty-something attendant at Corona Tower's Stamford Suites pool, rang early on the phone the next morning.

"Garik, good morning. This is Kofi at the pool. How are you this morning?"

"Still in bed." Garik hadn't identified himself. Talk about personal service. He pictured the sunlit pool where he, Marisa, and Kevin Lee had enjoyed part of a summer afternoon. Kofi Mandela had been as charming as every other Corona Tower employee, and friendlier than some.

"Welcome back. We are so glad to be able to offer you our extended Corona Tower experience. Your schedule today indicates lunch with the Director. That gives us several hours free. The workout facilities and the pool are available all morning. What time would you like me to arrive?"

"Arrive." Garik, still in bed, glanced toward the room's glass wall fronting Bay City. Moisture glittered at the edges of the glass, proof that it was cold outside. He understood Kofi's call and the reason Rodheimer hadn't felt it necessary to give his passkey full access to the building. He was to have babysitters, though apparently ones that were less obtrusive than Devon had been in the basement facility. "I haven't had breakfast. After that, maybe?"

"Certainly. If you would like, I can place that order now. Any preferences?"

"Is there anything in my kitchen? I didn't look last night."

"The inventory shows your kitchen has the upgraded package. It should include—"

"Just milk and cereal. Okay? Tell me that."

"Yes, you will have milk and cereal. I'll be there about nine. You will be ready?"

"Nine it is."

"Thank you, Garik, and enjoy your breakfast."

The phone disengaged, and Garik set it down. Kofi had been extremely pleasant and eminently helpful, but Garik understood perfectly well. His passkey and this apartment didn't give him freedom. His days were to be sliced and diced, monitored by Tower personnel and overseen at every moment. Cameras in the apartment? Audio recordings? Who knew—likely in the corridors and the elevators, but he shouldn't have any expectation of privacy even in the apartment, except hopefully in the bathrooms. And those were areas he could easily inspect for intrusive devices.

He threw back the bedding, grateful for his pajamas, and he yawned, felt his back pop, and stepped to the window. He found blinds overhead tucked into a hidden pocket and understood the remote he had found in the bedside table. The city was blanketed by fog, the Tower a fist thrust into the clouds, the home of the gods, according to mythology. Bored, he turned toward the bathroom, taking in the sharp nothingness of the bedroom's overly scrubbed air. Halo Sunchaser had once said the Tower guaranteed the purest and most odor-free environment possible. He believed her. He caught only the musky tang of the night's rumpled bedding and the citrusy residue of the previous evening's shower on his skin.

One thing he did appreciate. Kofi's call, his warning, rather. He hadn't just appeared at nine, wandered in, and expected Garik to muster to, shipshape and all that. Instead, he was getting The Corona Tower Experience.

He closed the bathroom door, looked around for anyplace a camera or microphone could be hidden, and didn't find any. Satisfied, he ran a hand over his bristly scalp, hit the sink faucets, leaned over, and splashed water over his face.

Patting his face dry, he studied himself in the mirror, the water running down his chest, his hands holding the towel. He was different, wasn't he? If he still had any of his old clothes in Irina's apartment, he wouldn't be able to wear a one. His arms had thickened, his shoulders likewise, and his height. Even the light switches forced him to reach lower. Still, his eyes were the same, clear gray speckled with gold, except for the eyeshine, and that was only noticeable when the lights were low.

"Bright lights," he said to the face in the mirror. "That's the solution."

His mood brightening, he tossed open the bathroom door and made his way to the kitchen, flipping on the lights as he entered, wondering what sort of cereal he would find.

"GYM FIRST," Kofi said as he inserted his passkey and the elevator doors closed. He smiled, warmly friendly. "That will allow you to freshen up at the pool before meeting Mr. Rodheimer. Your breakfast, did you find everything satisfactory?"

"Crunchy oats, yes." Garik was in workout gear, trainers and shorts underneath a thin track suit. Kofi had pulled a garment bag from the closet and selected an outfit for after their morning session. *For the Director*, he had said with a smile. Kofi carried it across one arm.

"Did you visit our gym when you were last here?"

"Not this one."

"We only have the one." Kofi chuckled as though Garik's reply was a joke. "Kevin Lee used it on occasion when training Ms. Sunchaser. I believe you were here with Kevin."

"And Marisa." The memory burned itself into Garik's eyes, and he blinked it away.

"Yes. I have heard. You were friends. I'm sorry for your loss. It's the disruption in the city. Perhaps we can get back to normal soon. You and I are likely to be the only ones using the facilities this morning. Not many guests just now."

It came to Garik that Kofi truly had no idea of the basement research facility. For him, the Tower stopped at the mall, and if there were storage facilities beneath that, they were none of his concern. A world existed in the Tower's basements, and it was hidden so well that even the Tower's aboveground employees were unaware of it.

What if Garik let it slip, suggested to Kofi that

things weren't as he thought, that there were hybrid mutant not-quite-humans now wandering the city, and they had been crafted right under his feet? Then he let his eyes search the nooks and crannies of the elevator and knew he wouldn't. Too many places for cameras and microphones. The first word and the elevator would freeze, Brace's paramilitary goons would drop in through the ceiling of the car, and bedlam would break out.

Kofi didn't deserve that. He was a good guy, earning a living at an honest job, and Garik felt the need to protect that. He recalled something he'd once thought during a conversation with Rodheimer. *Protect the family, protect the pack, take care of those under his care.*

Was Kofi under his care? He didn't see how, but he didn't want him to suffer because of him. He did notice that the man smelled of sun and water with a faint hint of coconut. A good smell, a pool attendant's smell. He decided he liked Kofi and he wanted to play the game for him, at least for the morning.

"YOU'VE BEEN putting in some gym time." Kofi offered Garik a towel. The man was unruffled in his Corona Tower polo and shorts, with his hair crisply clipped to imitate braided rows. He carried a tablet and tapped on it as Garik progressed through his workout.

"Not as much as I should, apparently." Garik was

battered, and he accepted the towel and wiped his face. What had happened to easy? Kofi kept upping his expectations until he saw Garik starting to struggle.

They hadn't been alone in the gym. A blond man Garik recognized, Boris Lindemann, the founder of Lindemann Airways, arrived midway through their session. His hair was no longer blue tipped but his face was the same, and Garik remembered what Kevin had once told him. *"Lindemann likes to tell people that there's something going on in the sub-basement."* Little did the man know how right he was.

Lindemann called, "Hey, Kofi," waved and moved to one of the treadmills.

"Good morning, Mr. Lindemann," Kofi replied, ending the interaction.

Lindemann left at some point without Garik being aware. He was more concerned with the kettlebells and making sure he didn't release one by accident and damage something or kill Kofi. Later, at the pool, Kofi became a drill instructor. Diving was with a resistance belt, foam dumbbells, strap-on weights. The more Garik proved he could do, the more Kofi insisted he do.

"I thought you were the pool boy," Garik panted as he pulled himself from the water to sit on the side of the pool. He realized the difference in this and his training with Christian. Christian had let him train at his own pace. Kofi was setting the pace.

"Competitive college swimming." Kofi grinned.

"And I've been told to challenge you. Are you challenged?"

"I shouldn't have tried to impress you." Garik stood, lifted a towel from a chair, and began to dry off.

"Not if you wanted an easy morning. We have an hour before lunch. How much time do you need to shower and dress?"

"I can take time for this." The pool was just them, and Garik tossed his towel to the side, wrapped an arm around Kofi's torso, and vaulted him into the water.

Kofi came up sputtering. "What was that for?"

"Trying to impress you. I'm ready for that shower now." He grinned, retrieved his towel, and headed off to prepare for lunch with the Director.

SCRAWLED ACROSS a faux stone-and-cedar wall in black iron and backlit with a soft white glow, Stamford Suites Grill welcomed Tower guests to an *exceptional dining experience.*

It said so right under the name, An Exceptional Dining Experience.

Ted Charles, the restaurant manager, greeted Garik at the entrance, taking over for Kofi. The transition was so smooth that it would have been seamless had Garik not known what they were doing.

"Good morning, Garik. You were here in the summer, I believe, on a tour with Gunther." Gunther Diehl was the concierge who had given Garik, Marisa, and Kevin a partial tour of the facilities.

"Yes, and you are Mr. Charles. I'm surprised you remember."

"It's my job to remember." He smiled. "This way if you will. The Director is already here."

Their table was nestled in a generous bay fronted by glass and a view towards the waterfront. This side of the building faced just to the northwest and the glass was protected from the sun. The room was warm but the water in the distance was winter gray and whipped by the wind. When Garik listened carefully, he could just hear it wail outside the building's glass walls.

Rodheimer invited him to sit, asked him about his morning, but didn't offer him a menu. Food arrived shortly without any further interaction with the wait-staff. The portions were impressive, with steak, chicken, and cod. On the side, cottage cheese and yogurt. Potatoes, asparagus, and two boiled eggs. Each.

"This is a lot," Garik said, as he leaned sideways for yet another plate to be added to the table.

"Big men require big meals."

Garik had never thought of himself as a big man. But Kofi had worked him hard, and the food was appealing. Still, even he couldn't consume the vast quantity he'd been offered.

Rodheimer ate with gusto, polished his plates, and called for dessert.

"I don't think I can," Garik said, pulling his napkin

from his lap and dropping it beside his plate.

"Then neither will I." He called, "Ted, no dessert. We're done here."

Garik caught Charles nodding, and when he raised his head to turn away, he locked eyes with Garik for a moment, and Garik remembered the tic from the previous summer. It was back. It hadn't been there when Garik arrived at the restaurant. But he couldn't decipher the clues and shrugged it off. He turned back to Rodheimer, "What's my schedule for this afternoon?"

"You've worked that out. I knew you were smart. You keep proving me right, and we'll make something of you yet. We're meeting someone. He's useless in his current condition, so I'm putting him to work. Be good to him this time."

Be "good" to him? What did that mean? He hadn't been "bad" to anyone.

Except Justin, and that didn't count. He wasn't in the Tower any longer . . . he hoped.

Absorb, understand, extrapolate. He should be able to predict this, but again, he had to let it go. He needed information to see the future, and that he didn't have.

— 6 —

arik found himself handed off to yet another keeper,
one that puzzled him.

Kang Song, the Tower's event planner and hospi-
tality head, a person he had *nearly* met on his first visit
to the tower BACK WHEN HE WAS AN UNMODI-
FIED HIGH SCHOOL STUDENT, appeared in the corridor outside the restaurant in a black suit with a white
banded collar finished out with diamond bracelets and

earrings.

"Good afternoon, Director." She nodded her head to Rodheimer slightly, whether in respect or deference was hard to say. Bypassing Garik slotted him into his order of importance. She continued to the Director, "Thank you for the opportunity to help you."

"I am sure you will handle this assignment beautifully, Miss Kang. Kofi is occupied for the afternoon, and it was inconvenient to alter his schedule. See that Mr. Shayk gets to the lobby with no side trips. If Charity isn't at her desk, I am certain Gunther will step in." He lowered his voice, "At no point is he to be unattended. Is that clear?"

"I will do all as you say." This time, she did bow, a slight bend of the waist, before she turned to Garik. "Good afternoon, Mr. Shayk. Do you prefer to use your last name or your first?"

"My first." He glanced at Rodheimer. "If that's okay."

The big man nodded. "One warning. I have obligations this afternoon so cannot intercede if there are problems. Colonel Brace isn't your biggest fan just now, so steer clear if you can. Miss Kang, thank you for your time. I know it is valuable to you."

He was gone, surprisingly quiet on his feet for his size. Garik thanked Ted Charles for lunch and was told, "Anytime, Mr. Shayk. Dine in or order up, the choice is yours. Let me know if you wish to dine in and are unaccompanied. I can provide a companion to retrieve you from your apartment."

Garik got it. He could dine in but not travel from the apartment to here without a handler. Very smooth.

"Shall we go, Garik?" Kang motioned with her hand, tinkling each time she moved. "If you wish, my first name is Song. Miss Kang if you prefer."

"Song. I like that. Who are we meeting?" The elevator doors closed them in, and the car barely seemed to move. In the scrubbed air, Miss Kang was vanilla and cherry blossoms, a pleasant aroma.

"I am afraid I do not know him. I am so sorry." She nodded her head in a bow, only slightly involving her shoulders. "Understand, I am event planner, but with the city, we have few events, so my time is free. I know many people here, but not this one." She smiled.

"Surely they told you his name." Someone he needed to be good to. Nothing in his head was coming through on that one.

"Oh, yes, I have him. His first name is De-Voon. I am unsure of his looks, however, so we must trust Charity to make us connected. Charity is Miss Cellers. You know her?"

"We've met." De-Voon. Garik tried to place a De-Voon. His mind was blank.

"Ah, I expected such. Thank you." She did her bow again. "Ah, we are here." The door dinged and opened. Miss Kang retrieved her passkey and they stepped out.

Charity was away from her desk and Gunther was nowhere to be seen. "We have a few minutes. I will take you on a short walkabout. We have exceptional facilities, the best in the city."

She led him through a wide doorway into the glass-walled atrium, pointing out the oversized artworks that leaped from the floor to proclaim, "Notice me!" and gave him a short history of the artists and how each one came to be in Corona Tower.

Garik listened but also thought of the Director's whispered, *At no point is he to be left unattended.* The instruction wasn't unexpected. The fact that he whispered it and didn't realize Garik would be able to hear it was.

So, Director, he thought. I might still hold a few surprises. Houdini, anyone? The third time will be the charm. Then his rainbows zapped his head, he missed something Miss Kang said, and she paused and turned to him expectantly.

"I'm very sorry to ask this, but is everything okay? Miss Cellers is waiting."

Garik pulled his head together, brushed aside the lingering endorphin rush the zap of rainbows had left behind, and focused on Miss Kang's words. Charity . . . waiting . . . and that meant De-Voon. He turned to locate De-Voon and was pleasantly surprised to find a one-legged blond man with a pronounced cowlick just visible at his left temple.

"De-Voon," Garik called, raising one arm to wave.

Devon Maye looked around, puzzled at the unusual pronunciation of his name, and paused when he caught Garik. He looked him up and down, as if evaluating whether this was the same person he'd spent time with only recently. He decided it was, shifted his crutches, and grinned.

"Get over here, kiddo. I'm your babysitter for the afternoon. How's that sound?"

"Like peaches and cream." Like a big brother, an old friend, someone he could trust. Yes, Mr. Rodheimer, I can be good to De-Voon.

Especially as the broken leg was one hundred percent Garik's fault.

WHILE THE city might be in disarray, the Tower's 10-Plex was fully operational and showing the latest films. Devon didn't have permission to allow Garik into the basement research center, so they decided on an alien shoot-'em up taking place on a distant planet.

"This might make the people I work with seem normal, eh, kiddo?" Devon chuckled as he hobbled to his seat. He could stand without his crutches, but the cast was heavy, and he couldn't bend his knee. The crutches were a convenience, and he left them at the door and chose a handicapped seat with extra space to stretch his leg.

"Makes me seem normal." Garik glanced at the

empty theater. Only three other people, and they were way at the back.

"Seriously? Have you looked in the mirror? And I don't mean just the new haircut."

"Several times." They were seated, and Garik placed two drinks between them. He also had a bucket of popcorn for snacking. He set it on an extra seat for later.

"I was taller than you the last time I saw you. Not any longer. I've been the activities director for a long time—" He started to say something else, paused, and sat up and looked around. The lights were dimming, and he relaxed into his seat.

"What?" Garik asked.

"Being careful. Up here, we have to watch our words."

"The confidentiality agreement. Kevin mentioned it once."

"Any new abilities?" Devon seemed amused. "Like being able to climb the wall all the way up? Heh, kiddo?"

"Maybe a few." Rainbows. Lots of rainbows. The film was rolling the intros by then, and he asked, "How are things down there?" Not in the "research center" but "down there." Devon would understand.

Devon shared that while the upper part of the Tower seemed normal, downstairs was a cauldron of distrust between the researchers, the hybrids, and the military.

Garik expected that. He'd only left the hospital shortly before. He learned the hospital on Level 4 hadn't experienced the worst of it. Brace had an iron fist on everything.

"Here's something you'll want to know, that is, I think you will." On the screen, an alien with claws for hands was ripping through the ship's hull to get at the beautiful captain who wasn't yet in her spacesuit.

"Sure. What?" Garik was enjoying the events in the movie, people in a worse situation than his. He tried to put aside that they could take off the makeup and go home to their families when the cameras stopped rolling.

"Kevin attended Marisa's funeral. It was held at St. Anne's. Her parents told the crowd that Marisa had been visiting and drawing pictures of the paintings on the ceilings, and they knew she loved the old building."

Marisa. Garik squeezed his eyes shut, trying to dam the moisture about to spill over. Even with his eyes closed, color ricocheted in his head, his heart raced, and his lungs swelled with air. The anger at what had happened wrestled with him, tried to take from him what he refused to give.

"Garik, dude!" Devon hit him hard on the knee with a fist. "What are you doing?"

"Doing?" Garik fought his lungs, his heart, the rainbows. He forced his anger inside, sealing it away, repeating to himself, *Anger gets me nothing. My mind.*

My desire. My way.

"The arm of the chair. Look at it."

Garik opened his eyes, looked down, and found he held the arm of the chair, but it was no longer attached to the floor or to the side of his seat. The handle revealed the imprint of his grip on the wood.

And his seat was canted, completely unattached on one side.

"The seat on your other side is free. Maybe I should move there." Garik leaned the arm against his seat, collected the popcorn, and shifted to the new location.

Devon leaned in, "How much *have* you grown?"

Garik tried to focus on the film, the aliens slicing up the ship section by section, but Devon wanted to know everything . . . about him . . . about what had happened to him . . . where he'd been after disappearing from breakfast. Part of it Garik didn't mind sharing. Some of it was too horrible. And the worst he could only hope wasn't true, like Paul and John lying crumpled on the parking garage floor, unmoving and lifeless.

Then the aliens began to eat the remaining crew members, and for a short time, Garik's problems faded into the background, and not even Devon had any questions for him. The aliens were truly nasty, almost as bad as some of what the Tower's research center had unleashed on Bay City and the world.

GARIK FINALLY worked up the courage to ask about

Dieter and his brother, Luka. They were his biggest fear. The brothers were innocents in a battlefield of committed assailants, and he was afraid for them. He'd experienced the terror and despair of the worst that life could throw at him, and he wouldn't wish that on anyone else.

"Well, I lost the opportunity to drive Dieter anywhere—"

"As if you could." Garik tapped the cast with his shoe.

"Right-o, kiddo, but even if I could." Devon shifted position before continuing. "His dad hired a car to drive him—"

"His brother, Luka, the chauffeur. I met him."

"You know more than I do, then." The movie was at the end, with loud music and ending bloopers popping up to keep people in their seats for the final credits. Devon took a last sip of his drink before handing it to Garik to drop in the trash bin.

"Hardly. Are they okay?"

"Your guess." The lights were coming up, and Devon shrugged. "I visited the apartment, and it was vacant. Gunther said something about their father's treatment taking them to Galveston."

"Texas." Garik tried to picture what he knew about Galveston.

"I think they have a big cancer hospital there, likely a better treatment facility. At least we won't forget

Dieter." Devon tapped his cast-covered leg and grinned.

"Right." Garik dropped the empty drink containers in the bin and retrieved Devon's crutches. He knew why the brothers had left, and it was nothing to do with a better treatment facility. Dieter's broken hand at Rodrigo's forceful push. Garik's unexpected rainbows forcing them into the cold. The limousine destroyed by Brace's hybrid goons. They had run for safety, their father willing to trade his health for his sons' protection. His sons were safe, no matter if he gave up every other thing that was important to him, even his life.

Where did Garik fit in that formula? Was he the son that needed protecting or the protector willing to sacrifice everything for those under his care?

Information. Evaluation. Extrapolation.

He didn't want to extrapolate. He wanted to wipe every path from his future, have just today, enjoy the moment without seeing it change the options branching out in front of him in a spaghetti tangle of impossible "what ifs."

"I'm ready," Devon said, pulling himself to his feet. "Good movie, by the way."

"The best," Garik chimed in. And no werewolves involved. He would take what he could get, and for no werewolves, it had been more than worth his time.

— 7 —

arik ran on a treadmill. In front of him, the glass wall. Beyond that, a series of names he had come to know and either respect or dread.

Colonel Brace, the de facto person now in charge of the human-hybrid project, even if his power was due to the force of his paramilitary hybrid forces and the money wielded by the U.S. and Canadian coalition of Armed Forces that funded the project.

Airman First Class Wu Han, whom Garik knew and had formed a bond with even before he knew about the Tower's secretive DNA-melding experiments. He sat just behind Colonel Brace and next to Second Lieutenant Ron Wilder, whose arms looked like they could break bricks.

Senior Airman Shan Vang sat on the other side of Wu Han, wearing a strawberry face and Cambodian eyes. He presented a mannerly, polite demeanor, but Garik knew otherwise.

Master Sergeant Megan Valladao, whom Garik had found supportive. She backed Brace and his policies, but she was mostly unknown to Garik. He had interacted politely with Valladao, but he didn't yet trust her.

Garik knew Major Judy Kennedy and Captain Ryan Lee from their escort service when Director Rodheimer and Colonel Brace had demanded to see him. At the time Rodheimer and Brace were still nominally on the same team, but the lines had been drawn that day, Air Force personnel under Rodheimer's oversight or the hybridized soldiers supported by the funds to which Brace held the drawstrings. Brace's hybridized paramilitary goons had won the draw, but for how long? Kennedy and Lee were on Brace's side of the bleachers.

Three more Air Force support personnel lined the back wall, standing. Garik knew them by title but little else. Airman Ronisa Kim, computer specialist; Airman Megan Franke, warfare specialist; and Airman Molly

Biggs, senior logistics coordinator.

They had come to see him sweat and outperform in every quantifiable statistic they could come up with. Could he run farther, maintain his endurance longer, be the super soldier they hoped him to be?

The standard was high. Brace's paramilitary goons could do everything they had asked of him. They expected more of Garik.

And yet, and yet . . . Garik understood who he needed to impress, that his true test didn't come from Brace or his covey of tittering birds.

The true evaluators on the other end of the scoreboard held the placards they could raise either giving Garik their approval or condemnation. Approval meant he lived to labor another day. Condemnation was a one-way ticket to Level 5, the basement floor that said you were on the way out, perhaps even to be dismembered for further research purposes.

Director Rodheimer with his massive shoulders took up the space of two men. Occasionally, he glowered at Brace, but his expertise had kept him in charge of running the program.

Halo Sunchaser had been in attendance early, but she had disappeared with a scowl at Garik's ever-improving scores, especially when Rodheimer had seemed pleased.

Senator Gleeson Arcady was new to the mix. He had arrived after the blowup between Rodheimer and

Brace. Large—tall as well as wide—with a polished head, the man carried an unlit cigar and dismissed people by placing it in his mouth. He seemed shady to Garik, and he wondered what the man had over others that kept him in power.

Also from the Tower's retinue, Annie Vanschooneveld, the foreign affairs attaché. It seemed surprising to see her without Devon, but then, Garik had never seen her in her official position. She had winked at him and given him a smile at the beginning of the day.

Last, Michelle Winn, the staff development and personnel coordinator. Garik assumed she was present to fill a chair, more to bolster Rodheimer's numbers than to do anything helpful.

Garik continued to run, his eyes watching the watchers, unconsciously extrapolating what would likely happen next. Brace and Rodheimer had crossed swords earlier. Rodheimer was still convinced Garik had precog tendencies, and Brace had laughed it off, saying his hybridized paramilitary were the direction to go. Why was this one punk worth their time? All Brace required was a genetic fix for oxygen absorption and he would have the soldiers he needed.

Of course, none of that happened in front of Garik, or to be more precise, not *directly* in front of him. They had been out of sight but not out of hearing, not yet clued in to how well he could hear. Now, Garik gave them nine-out-of-ten odds they would come to words over it, and Brace would demand Garik prove himself against his hybrid goons. As if that wasn't what the incident in the underground garage had already done. Garik had bested them all, well, with Jantzen's help, and two of his friends had been taken down, but Garik hadn't known it was a fight to the death until it was already underway AND he was suffering under a DNA-triggered deficiency that was now supposedly repaired.

He ran, not out of breath, not tired. Perspiring, but that was his body adapting to the demands he placed it under. He tracked his predictions for Brace's blowup and knew he was within his fifteen-minute window for accuracy, his "precog" window, and could now even predict the men Brace would choose to battle him. Rodrigo, for sure, and he would likely choose from Jameson, Hyatt, and Simpson. The three goons Garik had taken out in The Martial Arts Center—Jenkins, Alberts, and Welling—were unlikely to be back in fighting trim. The men who had been with Rodrigo in the garage? They would be amped to smash face, likely with upgraded hardware and out for Garik's skin.

Brace finally raised his handset and barked, "Enough of this. We know the subject can run forever. I want to see him best some real men. Suit him up and get him onto a training mat."

The man stood, intentionally not looking at Rodheimer, and turned to exit the room. Garik thought, *real men*. Just on time, Colonel. I have your number down.

"THIS IS what the man doesn't know you can do."

Rodheimer had dismissed everyone from the ready room. He had out a tablet and he tapped play. The garage as seen from a security camera played. Garik was there, Rodrigo fired his weapon, and Garik blurred. Then he was standing in front of Dieter and his brother, and he slumped before blurring again and appearing before another man, this time blocking the view, but he seemed to take a hit before coming to his feet once more.

And that nearly killed me, Garik thought. I didn't have control of it, and it nearly killed me. Now I'm in control, but I don't dare go there again. I don't know what triggered that, and I don't want it to be triggered again. The jolt of electric rainbows eating at me inside, feeding me endorphin highs to convince me to do it again. Rodheimer thought they had resolved that with their upgraded DNA infusion. Yet, it still thrummed in his head, a string plucked over and over, so often it had become his nights and his days and his mealtimes and part of who he was.

Thrum. Surge. Ah, the endorphin high, then after a time, thrum, surge, endorphin high. Over and over, each time with a cymbal crash of electric rainbow, like a puddle of oil-infused water and a dinosaur walking in the distance. The water vibrates with each step, the oil shimmers on the surface, beautiful, but you know something deadly is on the way.

"It looks impressive," Garik admitted. "You people fixed that." Or so they thought.

"You are faster than anything we've managed so far, exactly what we've strived to achieve. Look at your clothing. You can barely fit, and these were custom made for you on your arrival. We must get your body rescanned, determine the growth rate."

"New clothes would be nice." His had been too snug recently, especially in the thighs and shoulders, and some in the length of his pants. He didn't feel taller or bulkier, but the proof was in the fit.

"You can outthink anything Brace's men throw at you. Keep that in mind. You are better than them." He sounded almost proud.

"His hybrids, you mean."

"Men." Rodheimer took a deep breath, as if making an announcement he had worked on over and over yet never had an opportunity to share. "You and me, we are men, above all else. Improved in many ways, yes, but fully men. Never forget that. You will be fighting hybrids who are men, nothing else. And they have a fatal flaw, one that requires them to wear an oxygen concentrator. Breaking it won't kill them, but they become ineffectual. Keep that in mind. Outthink them in every way. It's the one thing they cannot do. Think."

Think. Garik pictured the fight in the garage. He had achieved dominance only by use of his incredible speed. Was it possible to edge just close enough to use it but not give in to it? To stand on the rim of the black hole and not fall inside?

To fly like the gods and not have his wings burn up when he was too close to the sun?

It seemed he had no choice. Rodrigo was good, and if the others were allied against him, it was a fight he might be challenged to win.

GARIK WISHED he weren't so correct all the time, that his evaluation skills, his "precog" talents, weren't so close to infallible.

They were on Basement Level 3 in the recreation area. A large area was cleared and the floor marked off with boundaries. Across from Garik were his opponents, standing shoulder to shoulder with their helmets off and resting in the crook of one arm. Luis Rodrigo stood in the center, an even height with the three men alongside him. Rodrigo was dark with piercing eyes that said, *You've betrayed me twice, little man, but not a third time.*

Samuel Jameson had a scar on his face, with wiry blond hair. Huey Hyatt was more freckle than face, and Wally Simpson held his nose high, an aloof Roman god chiseled from stone.

All were decked out in paramilitary black, with the de rigueur stylized white eagle on their sleeves. Their legs were tree trunks, their arms logs, and their necks thick columns of impenetrable strength.

Garik wasn't so sure this was a good idea. Yet, as his opponents began donning their helmets, their visors hiding their eyes, and their hockey puck breathers taking the place of normal lungs and oxygen infusion through red blood cells pumped by the heart into the chest cavity, Garik felt his own heart triple its blood-transferring capacity, a repeated tympani thump in his chest moving faster and faster. His lungs swelled with more air than the room seemed to contain, and his hearing. *He could hear them speaking into their internal microphones.*

"Hyatt, left, use your knife. He doesn't have one. Cut a tendon, any tendon."

"Understood."

"Jameson, I'll feint after Hyatt, then I'll go right, confuse him. Stunner ready. I want him to die at my hands."

"Ready."

"Simpson, be my backup. Track what I do. If I don't get him, I want you to slice the icing from the cake. Electroknife charged?"

"And safety off."

Garik tracked the four of them. To the side, Brace glowed with confidence. The man knew his goons were cheating. He had selected the men, the weapons, and the charged situation to motivate them. It locked into place how Paul had managed to get the colonel's keys to his SUV so easily. The man had known, planned it all along, and had reprimanded and demoted Rodrigo just for this purpose.

Brace wanted Garik to die, and he wanted it public and with Rodheimer as a witness. Anger burned the rainbows hot, and Garik wanted to give in, give in so badly. The room burned with them, they encircled the para-goons; and even Brace, Rodheimer, and their collection of slimy eels bled vibrant rainbows.

The world in Garik's head vibrated with the need to release the rainbows and smash some goon faces. And yet, he knew that to do so was to reveal more than he wanted Brace or Rodheimer to know. He must skirt the black hole, skim the hurricane, slide down the rainbow to get to the pot of gold at the end. And so, with his grip tightly on the rainbows, he moved quickly, but not so quickly as to freeze time, just blur it a bit, confuse his opponents, remove the knife from Hyatt's sleeve, the stunner from inside Jameson's tunic, and the electro-knife from the collar of Simpson's boot. He wasn't sure what weapon Rodrigo carried, and he had to step into his circle three times to find it. A contact stun-stud mounted on the man's wrist, just where he could slam it against Garik's skin at any exposed point, slowing him as he took him out.

Garik lined the weapons along the floor just inside the marked boundaries. His last move was to disable each of the breathing masks. They were sturdy, but with a firm twist, he broke the contacts that enabled the exchange of oxygen-thin air to nearly pure gas and, he hoped, completely cut off the men's airflow through the masks. When finished, he stood beside the confiscated weapons, his arms crossed, and he listened to the men behind him crumple to the floor, forcing their helmets from their heads and leaving them clawing at their throats. Garik had seen this, too. They could breathe fine at normal activity levels, but their bodies were modified to operate at extreme levels closer to what he could achieve. Without their breathing masks, their muscles were starved for oxygen within moments.

Colonel Brace leaped from his chair, clearly not following Garik's moves. He cried, "Not possible! This is ... Rodrigo, get up! What are you men doing? Jameson, Hyatt, Simpson, say something, men!"

"Can't ... breathe, sir." Huey Hyatt's freckles had blended into one solid red face, and he was on his knees, pulling at the chest of his clothing, trying to undo it for more air.

"Get your helmet on, Hyatt!"

"Broken, sir." Samuel Jameson could at least speak. He held up his helmet. "The end is twisted nearly off."

Rodrigo and Simpson pawed at their helmets until they found the air transfer devices and discovered that, yes, theirs were the same.

"How—" spluttered Brace, infuriated. He turned to face Rodheimer. "This is you, Director. What tricks have you played to embarrass me like this?"

"Garik," Rodheimer called, clearly pleased with the outcome of things, "what's that at your feet?"

"Hyatt had a knife up his sleeve. Simpson had an electroknife in his boot. The stunner is from Jameson's tunic, and Rodigo wore a contact stun-stud on his wrist. It's not there any longer."

"I suspect not." He turned to Brace. "I played the one thing that could best your men, even with the surprises you evidently asked them to carry to ensure their victory. Your men are no match for what I can offer the world."

Garik glowed with his success. He even chose to overlook the Director's final words. *For what I can offer the world.* With his anger unleashed, he had felt powerful—and free of the torment of losing Marisa, his family, his friends, and his entire life.

Just for those few moments, he had felt like he was back in control once more.

— 8 —

arden. Guard. Sentry. Escort. Chaperone.

Handler.

Garik had no misconceptions, wore no blinders, looked through no rose-tinted glasses. For the next few weeks, he was restricted to the few places his passkey would allow him to go or was in the presence of one of his Tower minders.

Yet, his resentment faded. Many of his custodians,

such as *De-Voon*, cracked jokes with him, sometimes teased, and felt like real friends. Others—Kofi, Gunther, Song, even Choi Bak on one occasion—were polite and unobtrusive, showing up, fading into the background when necessary, and making the transition from handler to handler seem as fluid as oil flowing across water.

Kevin Lee appeared at his door early one morning. He wore a lightweight track suit with dark banding at the wrists and waist. He grinned and held out a package, folded cloth wrapped in a contrasting cloth belt.

"Good morning, Kevin." Garik yawned and accepted the package. "It's too early for the day to start, but come in."

"Fancy place." It was Kevin's first time alone with Garik since his return, and he hadn't visited the apartment.

"Yeah, boring with no one around." Garik set the package on the counter and opened the fridge. He was just up and still in his nightclothes and barefoot. His torso was uncovered, and the light from the fridge revealed how much he had changed since his return to the Tower. Around his face, his hair now looked like real hair, long enough to begin to curl although not long enough to have any real dimension. It had been trimmed twice around his ears and the nape of his neck.

"Thanks," Kevin snorted, noisily sliding out a chair and sitting at the table.

"What?" Garik pulled out a plate of fruit. He was constantly hungry, something Dr. Jimenez had assured him was normal as his body transitioned from youth to man. Garik had pictured his words differently. In his mind, youth to man became human to wolf-hybrid-thing.

"I'm a no one." He chuckled, tapping the tabletop. "Open that."

"Okay. You hungry?"

"Apparently not as much as you. C'mon, we've got plans, and I'm scheduled for lessons later this morning. Devon's improving but he's still a slacker. I can't depend on him to absorb my caseload."

"So why are you here? I'm not kicking you out, mind you, but it's usually Kofi this early, especially when he can't change his schedule for me."

"Because Kofi can't do this." Kevin stood, threw off the jacket to his track suit to reveal the top of a snug singlet encasing a tight, athletic frame. He crouched, raised one arm, and slashed it down, calling out, "Ai Kee!"

"We're going there?" Out of the Tower, Garik meant, not believing it possible.

"Now who's dreaming?" Kevin pushed the cloth package a few inches closer. "Open it and tell me you like it. It's sized to your latest body scan."

Garik set his apple aside and pulled the package to him. It would be clothing, then. He'd been forced to upgrade his wardrobe two times since being back in the Tower, each time requiring a complete replacement of every item. His height had settled at just under six-four, but his shoulders and shoe size refused to do the same. His neck was now a stovepipe, and he shaved daily. Wolf boy, indeed, forced to shave off his DNA heritage each morning to appear as a human being.

He shook out the package to find a loose, long sleeve jacket and matching pants.

"I'm guessing training this morning?"

"My treat. I invited you to Ai Kee! and then you had to get yourself tied up in all this. I have decided there's no time like the present."

"And they gave you permission—"

"Mr. Rodheimer jumped on it. Best all-around training a soldier can get—" He cut off his words. "Sorry. I know you don't like the soldier thing."

Garik shrugged. He lifted a black item wrapped in clear plastic. "This?"

"Compression shorts in your size. Guaranteed."

"Part of the uniform?" He ripped open the plastic to reveal mid-thigh, shiny fabric banded with white stitching.

"No, but you might appreciate that better than the old-world alternative." Kevin laughed. "Get changed. Let's see how quick you pick up on what I'm already really good at. Like Neo, download into your brain, zap, zap, martial arts expert."

THE REAL training equipment was in the basement, and with Kevin as his monitor, Garik tagged along. The chaperoning was seamless, with Kevin remaining almost within touching distance, whistling under his breath occasionally, mentioning that it had felt like it was still winter outside on the way in that morning.

Still winter outside. There were balconies Garik could access, though with his minders, he rarely did. Looking through his windows, there was a hint of green across the city, and he knew he would soon lose sight of City View Apartments. Then, he had nothing there, nothing except memories. Even Irina, his aunt. Arik had made it clear he was no longer welcome.

It was still early, and in the sunless basement, few people were out. Kevin had allowed that many people did wear tees under the uniform jacket, so Garik had pulled on the black shorts, found a black tee to match, and tied the jacket with the contrasting cloth belt. His shoes were black, lightweight kick trainers that were more slipper than shoe. His heavier shoes were off to the side for when they finished their training.

Partway through their training session, Stephen Klandermans appeared, easily recognizable with his kinky blond dreadlocks. He had shed his tattered clothes and boasted broad shoulders under a fitted, patterned tee and black shorts with Kick It in lime green letters on the front. His socks picked up on the lime, and his shoes were vivid yellow. His workout bag matched the black and green.

"Hey, Garik!" Stephen walked to the edge of the mat. He smiled broadly. "That's your face, but where did you get that body? I want one of those."

"Hey back, Stephen." Garik waved, and Kevin took the opportunity to turn Garik's lack of attention into a lesson and flipped the bigger man onto his back. Garik hit hard and lay panting.

"See?" Kevin knelt at his side. "Never look away. Even for an old friend. Let's take a short break."

"If you want. I know I do." At least until his back stopped hurting.

"Am I an old friend?" Stephen called, walking up, laughter in his words as he looked down at Garik.

"Not anymore." Garik shifted, in one motion came to his feet, and he straightened his sleeves. He was surprised how tall Stephen *wasn't* anymore. And his smell, the crisp aroma of arctic ice. Clear, pure, nothing else.

"I see they finally decided you were good enough to train with Kevin. He's unrelenting. Has he taken you to the wall, yet? He's now timing us. The last one up gets to clean the changing rooms."

"Maybe I should avoid the climbing wall." Garik missed this, people. One at a time was great, but he had lost something without a familiar river of people flowing through his life.

"Ineke is on her way. She's helping me with my gymnastics technique. Will you be here long? She would enjoy seeing you. And if not, well, I will enjoy seeing her see you." Stephen laughed. "See, there's Benjamin. Will he wave? Likely not. Benjamin!"

Ineke Van Stekelenburg was a hybrid modified with an ant for strength. Garik had never seen her spit formic acid—which he had been assured she could—but he knew she was strong. Benjamin Fuest, with caterpillar DNA, had clearly not undergone his metamorphosis stage, as he had demonstrated no skills at all. He hadn't yet been responsive to Garik in a friendly way.

Their attention shifted to a group entering the recreational area. Halo Sunchaser, in a mango headwrap and fresh green wraparound robe, emerged from a sea spray of aides and hangers on, the forefront of an incoming tide headed directly toward Garik in his martial arts uniform. Garik recognized Raymond Layton, the center's special events coordinator. He was surprised to see him on the training floor but supposed there was some cross-knowledge between many of the staff and the research fellows. Rachel Prager, who did clerical and data entry, carried a tablet and was dutifully entering as she walked. A man Garik identified as Jason Teague, although he hadn't met him and didn't know his duties, carried a slim case with a hinge on one end. Michelle Winn, with staff development and, Garik thought, the personnel coordinator, trailed the lot. He tried to make out their purpose here, when his thoughts began to turn like gears in an old-fashioned clock, and it clicked, the alarm going off.

This was about him. Sunchaser, disgruntled with Rodheimer's enthusiasm about Garik's apparent success. Layton, the man who would know that he and Kevin were down here training outside of Garik's regular training regimen. Rachel Prager, one of Jantzen's supporters, recording everything for the record, and Michelle Winn, likely to decide if Kevin had crossed a boundary that would require him to attend "staff development" courses to reacquaint him with Tower procedure.

Garik braced himself. He knew what was coming, could see it, and already grieved for the loss of something he'd only received a taste of: time with Kevin in a world that had been his home for much of the past year.

"Mr. Shayk," Sunchaser began, lifting her hawk-like nose and speaking crisply. "I see you don't feel the need to respect your boundaries."

"What boundaries? Kevin's with me. No alarms, and we have permission. Right, Kevin?"

"Ah, Kevin. This is not about Kevin. Let's not choose to blame him. I'm sure he thought he was doing the right thing. This is about you, Mr. Shayk. About your limits, your boundaries, your intrusion into your assumption of rights you do not possess. I would like to spell this out for you in the clearest way possible. Jason, if you will?"

Stephen had given them some space. Ineke had arrived, and they watched from a distance, trying not to be intrusive, but obviously listening to everything.

Benjamin, stalwart defender of his own interests, had vanished with the appearance of Sunchaser.

Kevin seemed mystified by all of it. He had asked permission, and the Director had enthusiastically approved.

Jason had a marker board unfolded, now sitting erect on its built-in stand. He held two board markers in his hand ready for use.

"A rectangle, Jason. The top for Corona Tower, and the bottom for where we are now."

"Just one?" He uncapped a marker, blue.

"One will do." Sunchaser nodded.

When he had it drawn, four easy strokes, he stepped back. Sunchaser took the second marker from him.

"This, Mr. Shayk, is your boundary, the line between your world and all of this." She stepped to the board and drew a red horizontal line to bisect the slender rectangle. She wrote *mall* on the line in neat, crisp letters. "Do you have a question, Mr. Shayk?"

He did, but he knew the answer already. He wanted to say, *I know who I am. You can quit calling me by my father's name.* However, she was making a point, and he shook his head no.

"Good. This is your world." She circled the top of

the tower in red. "This is not." She inserted a large red X on the portion under her line.

"That's it?" Garik could hardly resist laughing. It had hit him. She wanted Rodheimer to know how disgruntled she was. All this to make her point, to have it recorded, all her boxes checked. To discredit Garik in some sort of battle she was having with the Director.

Garik was her chess piece, and she would sacrifice him if necessary, as long as she won the game.

Garik hadn't yet figured out the game, but it would eventually come to him. Gather the information, sort the probabilities, extrapolate the outcome.

He had already sorted out one probability. Someone would suffer, and Sunchaser wanted it to be him.

— 9 —

fter Halo Sunchaser's vitriolic tirade, Garik fully expected to have every freedom stripped from him.

His passkey, his access to Stamford Suites Grill, the Tower pool privileges, even the martial arts uniform Kevin had provided him. He would be locked in, escorted from place to place with his hands bound, even his clothes given up for striped prison garb emblazoned on the back with Corona Tower. Danger. Approach at

Your Own Risk.

The only risk he proposed was the hole that would be left when he Houdinied out of this place. His run for freedom would generate a sonic boom of unreal proportions.

So, he asked himself. Why hadn't he already done that? He had received the DNA modification. His rainbows were under his control, if only marginally. What was keeping him here?

He understood the reasons even as he hated that he understood them. He was no longer the high school senior that had lost a summer, a fall, and a winter to the Tower. It was more than the months he had been out of circulation. His mirror said as much, reflecting back at him eight inches of height, and arms as thick as his legs used to be.

His old friends wouldn't know the person that hid in Garik's mirror, waiting to come out and mock him each time he brushed his teeth or took his razor to his chin.

And the other changes, the ones he could never talk about, never reveal. Kevin knew, and Devon, plus his hybrid friends, although most of them weren't in the Tower any longer.

The rest? He watched every word he spoke.

Kofi, well, Kofi was a great guy, but he didn't know about the human-hybrid project and what was happening just under his feet, and Garik wasn't the one to tell him. Nor Song, not that he could consider her a friend, but still, he did see her on a regular basis, and they had developed a distant but professional relationship.

Who understood him, could talk with him about what was really happening in his life? Dr. Jimenez? Unlikely. The man went into total meltdown if he wasn't addressed as Dr. Jamie. Nurse Ratchett? She thought of the hybrids as another mote in a petri dish. If it grew well, success! If not, toss it out.

Halo Sunchaser considered him the enemy. Jantzen had abandoned him, by necessity, but it still felt like abandonment. Paul . . . he had grown to like Paul, only to lose him in a gruesome fashion, and John, someone like him, gone, vanished, face-down and unmoving.

The rest of his friends? Even Dieter, someone he knew only through Ibn and Muhammad, vaporized in the heat of battle, cast aside, running to a safer place.

That left one person, Weston Rodheimer, a bear, er, gorilla of a man, someone who frightened everyone he was in contact with.

Except.

Except, except, except.

The Director had stood up for him in front of Colonel Brace. He had bragged on his skills, assured him he would continue to improve, even thought he had skills Garik knew weren't there. It might be a lie, but it was a lie that felt good, to be thought of as better than he was, to have respect, even if it was unearned and undeserved. To have someone whose eyes lit up when he walked in the room, who patted him on the shoulder, and when he penalized or restricted him, sounded as though it was the hardest thing he'd ever done.

A father figure.

Not a father. Garik had one of those, and he would never believe the Director if he said he cared about him. He wasn't sure the Director even liked him or wanted to spend time with him, and Garik knew he often didn't like the Director. Still, a pat on the shoulder, a kind word, someone who believed in him even when it wasn't warranted. Sometimes that was all life offered, and you took what you got.

"COME IN, Garik!" The Director's voice rumbled from inside his penthouse suite.

Garik stepped through the door. There wasn't a bell, and it had opened before he could knock. No one stood to greet him but the Director's massive voice.

He was in his best, grey slacks, polished brogues, a black silk shirt with deeper black woven stripes, a matching belt, and under it a black tee shirt with a label that said it cost more than every item of clothing he had owned back in his aunt's apartment. Gunther Diehl had joined him that afternoon, informing him that he was requested to freshen Garik's haircut, offer him a custom shave (clearly not an offer), and provide him a new outfit appropriate for the evening.

This was to be dinner with Mr. Rodheimer, and

Garik needed to be at his best.

"Thank you," he called, the politeness coming by reflex. His nerves were on edge, and his stomach churned. He did note how the entrance seemed smaller than the last time he was here. Tighter, the walls closer, the ceiling lower.

Or he was wider, taller, larger in every sense.

Rodheimer appeared, held out a meaty paw to greet him, and when Garik took his hand, the man uncharacteristically pulled him forward to clap him on the shoulder. Not a hug, but near enough that it startled Garik.

Father figure, he thought. Hardly. Yet, the action relaxed him, drew him in, gave him a sense of oneness with the man, an intimacy that Garik had with no one else. A false sense? Garik didn't look too hard. What one needed—and desperately—one didn't inspect too closely. If it didn't stand up to inspection . . . the letdown might be unbearable.

"Follow me a moment, my boy." Rodheimer released him, tilted his head to indicate the way, and started down a corridor. He led him into a wood-paneled room. A low couch in a nubby, pale green fabric stretched along one wall. A large painting above spoke to energy and color but no design that Garik could define. A wide desk, mostly empty except for a lamp and a writing pad. A wall of shelves packed with books.

"An office." Garik stated it plainly. The label asked why they were there.

"Mine, though used infrequently. Here is what I want you to see." He pulled out what looked like a book from a lower shelf but turned out to hold files. He removed a stack of photos, laid them out on the desk, not all fully visible. In one, a well-groomed man in his late twenties, no longer especially young, but his face still unlined. Garik realized it was the Director before he had undergone his DNA enhancement. Another, a woman by a ski lift. A mountain towered behind her. She looked pregnant. Garik pulled it out from the rest.

"My wife." Rodheimer touched her stomach. "My son. That was taken the day she—" He cut off his story and pulled out another photo, this time with the Director in a hospital bed hooked to lifesaving equipment. "This is what I want you to see."

"You. What was wrong with you?"

"I was first, the original of all of us. We had to begin somewhere, and when I lost Meg . . ." He stumbled on his words for a moment, then he took a deep breath and plunged ahead. "I was in that bed for six months. What happened to you put me there. Jantzen saved me. The man is brilliant if misguided, but that's beside the point. I was under sedation the entire time. I want to know, what was it like?"

Garik was surrounded by the man's aroma, the anticipation. This was why he had been invited this evening. This was something he needed to know, and it had been denied him.

"Intense," he said.

"You move, and it's as though you disappear and reappear. Relive that for me."

"It put me in the hospital. Your people topped me off with new DNA juice, and now it's over." He studied the picture, but the one of the man's wife was on the table, and he couldn't help glancing at it. He remembered Jantzen's story, that Rodheimer had lost his wife and changed. Maybe been driven to become the guinea pig for the program.

"But when it was happening? You must recall something."

"A little." It was still trying to happen. The DNA upgrade only helped him control it, and it would run away from him again if he let it. "You don't remember any of it, do you?"

"An opportunity missed." Rodheimer sorted through the photos, lifting out one occasionally. "But no, and I want to understand how it feels. Such speed!"

One of the photos showed a youth that looked like the Director, maybe fifteen, with a dark-haired boy of about the same age. Garik picked it up. It was outdoors, and a fire burned in the foreground. Rodheimer sat on a log, and behind him, the dark-haired boy had his arms under Rodheimer's, laughing and trying to pull him off the log. In that moment, Garik saw Jantzen with Justin in the ring, holding Justin's arms just like that to keep him from injuring Alyna with his knife-wielding hands.

"You and Jantzen. Why couldn't he tell you how he felt?" It was something Jantzen had said. He laid the photo back down.

"That is a very interesting question. What prompted it?" He lifted the picture Garik had held. "A long time ago. That was our last adventure in my father's old tent, when we knew, or at least I knew we didn't see the world the same."

"Okay, then don't tell." Garik shrugged, not really understanding why they were looking at images of Rodheimer's past life. Maybe to get him to open up, form a bond of intimacy between them. It took two to go there, and the Director didn't want to play. "I remember one thing about moving so fast."

Rodheimer dropped the photo of him and Jantzen, and he focused fully on Garik. "Tell me."

"It hurt really bad, every time I moved. It's not something I'd wish on anyone."

"No, I guess not." The Director didn't sound convinced.

THE TABLE was set for three.

Garik didn't think much of it, although later, he realized the pictures in the Director's office had jarred his brain. To him, Rodheimer had always been a big, broad-shouldered gorilla guy. To think of him as a normal guy with a wife and expecting a child, a son, readjusted everything about the man in Garik's head.

The third guest arrived just before they sat down to eat. The doorbell rang, Rodheimer tapped his watch, and he called, "In here, Halo. Perfect timing, as always."

Garik's stomach dropped. Why was she here? As she walked in, she seemed equally surprised to see him. Yet, her manners were impeccable, and she greeted them both, giving the Director an air kiss and taking Garik's hand and patting it once before releasing it.

The meal arrived in several courses. When Garik had trouble deciding on which utensil to use, Rodheimer chuckled and tapped the one farthest from his plate, saying, "Outside in. Never start next to the plate."

"Weston," Sunchaser said with a smile. "You're treating him like a—"

"Like a child?" Rodheimer snapped. "My apologies, Halo. We were looking through some old photos. My thoughts were still in the other room."

"Quite all right. I was going to say like a son, the way a good parent would do. You would have been a fine father if things had happened differently."

"Let it drop, Halo." The Director sighed, suggesting this was less a compliment than a jab for some unknown reason.

"You've even given the boy Jantzen's apartment. Like a good father would. When one son moves out of favor, the next one takes his place."

Garik remembered something the man had told Sunchaser: *I am not looking for a replacement for my unborn son.* Was that what this was all about?

"I never considered Jantzen my son. Let this rest."

"No, I don't suppose it was a father Jantzen wanted from you."

"Enough, Halo!" Rodheimer's hand hit the table and rocked the flatware. His skin sparked with static electricity. "Let's settle this now. You are not to interfere in my plans for this boy. I had hoped to be able to handle this gracefully, and you've not allowed that."

"And I will not allow him to usurp my place in this endeavor. Don't try to fill Jantzen's spot with this child. He is a child, Weston. Keep that in mind."

The tension eased and the meal continued, but Garik's mind was filled with two things. He was in Jantzen's apartment. Jantzen's! How special was that? And *boy?* Didn't they have eyes? The dining room blurred, the rainbows threatened, and the endorphins surged through his brain. Then, he steadied himself, picked up the next utensil and began the next course.

His head churned, however. Jantzen's apartment! His couch, refrigerator, bed! All Jantzen's! He could hardly eat for how excited he was.

$$— 10 —$$

arik fell into his bed, thinking, Jantzen's room.

Unless of course he had used the other bedroom, but still. He pictured evaporating into purple smoke and just *being in the kitchen in the morning*, no more walking across the apartment to get breakfast.

He killed the light, and with his wolfshine eyes, he studied the ceiling Jantzen would have studied. Once, he'd envied him being on the sign on Corona Mall, and now he was living in his apartment.

Better if Jantzen were here, but still exciting.

Garik dozed off, woke enough to turn on his side, kick at the sheets, and feel his breathing slow until he was hardly breathing at all.

Then the darkness in the apartment ate him up, swallowed him down, and welcomed him to the land of Nod where all dreams come true.

Especially the ones with wild wolf-boys, men who could morph into purple smoke, and other things that can only be formed from sealing wax and string.

STEPPING OUT of the apartment the next day, Kofi cautioned Garik that the Tower was under a bit of a strain.

"I needed special approval just to access the gym today." Kofi nodded as if that explained everything as he triggered the elevator, and they began moving downward.

Bit of a strain? Garik shrugged it off, still wrapped in his old mentor's apartment, imagining him watching television in the living room, heating up pizza in the microwave, brushing his teeth at the sink.

He paused. Did Jantzen watch television? He didn't know.

He understood Kofi's remark better when they exited at the gym. Tower security, the regular kind, not the Air Force or paramilitary, littered the building.

"Did anyone say why there are so many of them?" Garik watched them watch him as they walked, and he brushed off the feeling they were hoping to find trouble even if he was doing nothing wrong.

"Got me. Gunther approved our workout session, but we don't dare go anywhere but here. I have to call in now that we're here, then again when we're ready to leave. I'm sorry we can't do lunch or anything. Even the pool is off limits. The good thing is we can extend your workout session."

"Thanks," Garik said sourly. He pulled off his tracksuit jacket and tossed it onto a bench. Kofi picked up a gym phone just inside a small office. Garik dropped his carryall to the floor next to the bench and sat down.

Absently, he kicked off his shoes, slipped out of his tracksuit pants and tossed them after the jacket. He wore a gray tee, tight across the shoulders but loose at the waist, and black outer shorts over red compression shorts which ran almost to his knees. His socks were red against his black shoes. He put his shoes back on and stepped on a treadmill. He inserted the key and triggered the treadmill to elevate the walking deck and set the speed to five.

Garik had moved to the stationary bicycle and on to the rowing machine when Bom So-hye, Kang Song's secretary, with her hair a swirl of pink cotton candy, showed up at the door and motioned to Kofi. Garik continued to row, but he listened. Every word was perfectly clear to him.

"I'm sorry, Kofi. We have to clear the gym."

"I have Gunther's approval."

"I regret that this overrides everything else." She shrugged. "I told Song she should come tell you, because you wouldn't believe me, but you can call her if you wish. It is very quiet about this, so do not tell everyone." She glanced at Garik.

"No one knows we're closing the gym? It will be obvious when the door is locked."

"I just know what I am to say. There is a—" and she tiptoed, leaned in, and whispered, "—manhunt happening, and all security are asked to be on the mall."

"Manhunt!" Kofi glanced Garik's direction, and he turned back to So-hye. "Who are they hunting?"

"Shh." She put her fingers to her lips. "Jantzen Hefferly. Don't tell or I will be in trouble." She turned, waved coquettishly at Kofi, and left the gym.

Garik slowed his rowing for a moment, and when he saw Kofi look his way, he speeded up. His mind began clicking, a clock ticking the time, lining up the gears, and coming to a conclusion.

Rodheimer's unqualified approval of Garik and giving him Jantzen's apartment.

Sunchaser, clearly jealous, and ripping into Jantzen for some reason Garik couldn't define. Then there was her obvious anger that her place in the Tower's ruling echelon might be offered to someone else—in this case, him.

Now, they were on a manhunt for Jantzen. Even the word sounded like a tribal thing. Elephant hunt. Tiger hunt. Wolf hunt. Man hunt.

Garik would like to see his old mentor again, show off, let him learn how far he'd come. Jantzen had championed him when he was at his lowest, and he had been a friend to him when no one had seen how much he needed one. Look, he wanted to say, I'm in your old apartment. Look how much we're the same.

But manhunt. Who next, him? If Sunchaser caught Jantzen, would she stop there, or would she remove the next obstacle in her path to power?

Would the next manhunt be for him?

"WE HAVE to end our training session," Kofi called, and he carried Garik's bag to drop it beside the rowing machine.

"You promised extended time." Garik only slowed his workout slightly. He didn't want him to know he'd overheard. The longer he delayed, the more likely he was to find out additional information. Locked away upstairs, he'd learn nothing at all.

"Sorry. We have to get you back."

"I'm just getting warmed up." Garik laughed and gave the oars another strong thrust.

"Can't do. Sorry. This is from the top. Off." He

paused before saying, "Now."

"Sure. I can shower though, right? You can't expect me to wear this on the elevator."

Kofi looked toward the door, sighed heavily, and said, "Make it quick. If they do a building lockdown—" He felt of his passkey around his neck. "Just hurry."

Garik stripped his clothes and fell into the shower. Finished, he put on his clean things, stuffed the sweaty ones in the plastic bag in his carryall, and emerged with a bright look on his face.

"Hurry," Kofi said, already moving toward the door. "I don't want to be responsible—"

They were met in the corridor by two security who stopped them.

"Where are you two headed?"

"I'm delivering Garik to his apartment. He's at the top of the tower."

"Jantzen Hefferly's old apartment," Garik tossed in with a grin.

"So, you're the one under 24/7 supervision. Shayk's your last name, right?"

"Yessir, that's me." Garik said, bright and friendly.

"Are we okay to go?" Kofi looked hopeful. He pulled out his passkey to show he had one.

"Those are no longer working."

"I have Gunther Diehl's approval to be here—"

"You can have the Director's approval, and it's not getting you anywhere with that passkey. This building went into lockdown ten minutes ago. Come with us, you two."

The security team's passkeys did work the elevator. They dropped to the lobby to discover Charity Cellers' Front Desk vacated and several military types scattered around. None of Brace's hybrid goons were in place. Portable tables were erected, and everyone seemed to be in planning mode.

A cadre of men erupted from Rodheimer's office, with the Director in the midst of them, like something tasty surrounded by a cloud of hungry gnats.

"Director, if you have a moment," one of their security minders called.

"Yes—ah, Garik! Come with me." He motioned, and when Garik drew close, he placed his hand on the youth's neck and pulled him along, leaving Kofi and the two men who'd brought them to the lobby to fend for themselves.

GARIK FELT confused at first. The Director was organizing what seemed to be a citywide hunt for Jantzen. From their conversation the night before, he had been convinced Sunchaser wanted to punish Jantzen, but the Director was Jantzen's supporter.

Now, the man who had been Jantzen's boyhood friend pursuing him like a criminal? Why didn't they just let him go? He didn't know what to think.

As search teams across the city called in, Garik

knew they'd never catch the man. He was purple smoke, able to exit the smallest crack and reform into his physical self in any other location. The reports gave Garik a sense of pleasure.

"Team 6 at Fourth and Rock Island. Subject is headed south. Team 9, be set up and ready."

Subject. They meant Jantzen. They should just say it, but that's likely why they had the Tower in lockdown. They didn't want anyone to know what they were doing. Jantzen was well known, and if they were pursuing him publicly, the bad press could be devastating.

"Team 9 at Waddell and Fourth, ready to spring trap. We see subject now."

Jantzen was moving too quickly for him to be afoot, which meant he was in a car. Even in a car, he wasn't restricted from morphing. That meant he was driving . . . alone? If not, someone else could take over.

Unless they had used dart guns—or something worse—to disable everyone else in the car, forcing Jantzen to retain his solid form. If he were the only one able to man the wheel, he could be pursued until the car was brought to a halt. But even then, he would vanish in front of their eyes. How did they plan to get around that, force him to drive into a hermetically sealed building? That was likely impossible. How silly did they think Jantzen was? He wouldn't fall for any of their ridiculous shenanigans.

The radios lighted up again.

"Team 9, that's a no-go. Repeat, a no-go. Capture failed. Subject turning south on Ninth. Repeat, south on Ninth. Who's south on Ninth?"

"Team 4 arriving on Ninth. Stopping now. Repeat, stopping now. Setting up as I speak. Team 4 out."

Garik moved beside the Director. "What do they mean, setting up? What are they setting up?"

"Something I couldn't talk Halo out of. I know you looked up to Jantzen—"

"Looked up to?" Garik nearly hit panic mode.

"We don't think this will damage him too much—"

"He's your friend." Garik had seen the picture. The last camping trip. "You have to stop them."

"It is in process already. Jantzen could have stopped this before it began. Now, we're finishing what he started."

"What are they going to do to him?" He's your friend! Yet, Garik remembered what else the Director had said. They no longer saw the world the same. Jantzen had told him something similar. Whatever the reason, the Director was willing to let Sunchaser potentially damage Jantzen in some way to force him back into the Tower.

"We have theorized that we can prevent Jantzen's transformation from a solid to what is essentially a gaseous state through a pressure wave. It should interfere with the sublimation process."

"You'll kill him."

"Hybrids are pretty hardy. We can't be sure it will work, but it shouldn't kill him."

"How will you create the pressure wave?" Garik's heart raced, and he worked to control his breathing. No rainbows, not now. He needed to figure out a way to help Jantzen.

"Sonic boom derived from electrically induced lightning. It's why we've had to shut down Bay City."

"Everything's in lockdown?" They could do that?

"We've put the city under martial law. Colonel Brace has his paramilitary troops out in the city, and the Air Force is in pursuit. Tower security is filling in where necessary. The lightning we're producing is localized but strong. We don't need injury lawsuits."

Garik thought, *Jantzen, run! Evaporate, sublimate, whatever you've got to do.*

Use your rainbows if you have them.

Garik would offer him his, but he didn't see how they could help. He didn't know where Jantzen was headed, and in any case, he couldn't get there in time.

"Dear God, Holy Jesus in Heaven," he whispered. "Whatever you do, don't let Jantzen die."

Then the electronics in the room flickered, came back on full strength, and blinked out.

"Do we have him?" Rodheimer demanded.

In the darkness, no one had an answer to that.

he building's backup power supply jerked to life, indicators glowed, electronic devices clicked, and small machines made noises that said they were alive and breathing.

As screens illuminated and radios began to chirp, watches also began to glow. Somewhere in Bay City, a blown transformer had shifted power to a backup unit, industrial breakers the size of railroad cars had reengaged, and mobile devices and the Internet of all things were connected once more. The lights, now on, brightened, an indicator that city power had absorbed the load, and the Tower's basement power plant had returned to standby status.

A large screen showed multiple images around the city of traffic video feeds, several in color, most not. Some of the squares were blank, suggesting not everything was back online. A man worked a keyboard, searching though images that revealed empty intersections, with traffic lights blinking in neutral patterns, not yet fully operational.

No cars were on the streets, anyway. The larger military-type machines ignored the lights no matter what pattern they flashed.

"Where is he?" Rodheimer muttered.

Garik heard the emotion in the man's question. Concern. Respect. The frustration of a situation that shouldn't have been allowed to happen. Layers of anger washing over it all.

Finally, one scene caught the computer operator's eye, he took control of the camera, and he shifted it to pan the intersection. The image swelled to envelop three others, then it grew again to eat the entire screen.

"Enlarge. I wish to see detail."

The image zoomed past men packing up equipment with thick power leads, to reveal an SUV with the front left side crumpled around a power pole. Garik's mind involuntarily evaluated the possibility that the electrically induced lightning—the reason for the power leads—had created the power failure with its electromagnetic pulse, or whether the power pole strike had been enough to cause the damage. Gears clicked in his head, telling him that only an EMP could have wreaked so much damage. Everything had powered down, including things that should have been able to draw on battery reserves and continue working.

In the scene, now fully magnified, the camera revealed cracked plate glass in buildings. Windows hung limp in their frames. A section of curb was layered with concrete fragments, as though the street had rippled with the blast, and the surface had sheared away into dust.

How much power had they discharged to create a pressure wave that could disable Jantzen's ability to sublimate from solid to gas, to morph from man to mist, to escape any confinement that wasn't hermetically sealed?

How much did Sunchaser hate the man that she would risk the city to bring him home, even as she skirted his death?

In the image, they watched as men armed with weapons surrounded the vehicle. One tapped the cracked glass on the driver's door with the muzzle of his weapon, then he looked closer, took the door handle, pulled it, found it wouldn't open, and motioned to the men with him. One man got on a radio, and a siren began that they could hear even in the Tower. It was mere minutes before the scene began to strobe with the lights from an emergency response unit. During that time, other doors were forced open, and people were pulled from the vehicle. Giselle Harmon, modified with a sea cucumber and able to liquify and re-solidify. Julia Cantos, with her boa constrictor heat-seeking ability. Paolo Leveen, pistol shrimp modified and able to shoot boiling water from his fingertips and stun his opponents with sounds up to 200 decibels.

None were moving. What had happened to them? Dead—Garik couldn't think it, refused to let himself consider the possibility—but what else could he think?

Then the Jaws of Life, peeling away the roof of the SUV. The door hinges were cut away, sparks flew, and the door was tossed aside. More sparks from the interior, and they pulled out Jantzen, limp, with blood streaming from his ears and nose.

Garik was furious. How could they have done this? He fought the rainbows, clamped down on them hard, his head resonating with the clamor of their presence, repeating the mantra: my mind, my power, my choice. Anger never brings success.

Yet, that was all he wanted. He hoped beyond hope Sunchaser hadn't killed him. If so, well, he didn't know what he would do, but it wouldn't be kind. She had no right, *no right*. No matter what Jantzen had done, he didn't deserve to die.

The world blurred with color, and Garik struggled to keep it under control. Release the rainbow, his head cried. Yet, his will prevailed as the scene of horror continued to unveil before him.

"IS HE DEAD?" Garik knew he should be asking whether *they* were dead. They were all his friends, had escaped with him the first time he had broken free of the Tower's chains, and had done what he could not: remained in the city to effect change in the Tower's control over Bay City.

Yet, that one image washed out all the others, Jantzen, his ears bleeding, his body limp in the hands of his captors.

"Apparently not." Rodheimer's deep voice seemed amused. "Watch."

On the screen, two men appeared, and they opened a case with four circlets securely wedged into pre-formed foam inserts. They withdrew each one, keyed it with a remote, and it popped open. One was placed on each of Jantzen's wrists, and the other two found his ankles.

"Capacitors." Rodheimer sounded satisfied. "If the man tries to sublimate, they will sense it and release a charge to stop it."

"Built in pressure wave." Garik pictured it, the ultimate chains for a man that couldn't be chained.

"Not exactly, but it serves the purpose. Come, let's locate Halo. She has been at the forefront of this, and she will wish to be congratulated."

"You approve?" Garik was still in shock at what he'd seen and heard.

"Approve? Hardly, but it had to be done at some point. I understand your connection to the man. I felt the same myself at one time, but he was no longer thinking rationally. To throw away everything we've worked toward when we are on the cusp of success? When we have you as proof? I could forgive his short-comings, his penchant for softness toward those who couldn't further our ends, when he accepted my authority and bent to my will, but as you see, the man is no longer sane. He had no hope of success, yet he still ran. And for what? That?"

Rodheimer stepped to the screen and gestured to the three people carelessly dumped on the street, their bodies lined up but not in any way cared for. It was Jantzen they were after. The others didn't matter, or so it seemed.

Garik was gutted, his sense of right and wrong spilling from him unchecked and tangled. Rodheimer, for whom he'd developed a grudging admiration, and Jantzen, for whom he didn't exactly admit love, but the feeling was close. A mentor, a friend, a surrogate father who had been his lifeline, both figuratively and literally.

He watched the men give Jantzen a shot, wait a few moments, then slap his face, once, twice, then three times until he stirred. Garik's anger surged, his rainbows surged, and he felt time around him slow as he skirted the black hole just enough to see Jantzen on the screen become translucent, causing a spiderwire film of electricity to emerge from the circlets and encase his body. He went limp again, and the men attending him acted disgusted. Once again, Jantzen received a shot, and this time, he recovered quicker, after only one slap.

Trapped. The ultimate chains. A prison not even Jantzen could wriggle out of.

The humiliation must be crushing. Garik absorbed his pain, wishing to take it all, if he could.

THEY MET Sunchaser on the way to the hospital on Basement 4. Her hair was wrapped in camo green and her matching kaftan broken only by a vine of red flowers that bled down one side. Her eyes narrowed at Garik's presence, but she immediately warmed to Rodheimer. She took his hand and air kissed his cheeks.

"My dear Weston, a step forward. You must be pleased. The wayward prodigal is returned."

"Your doing, Halo. I would have chosen a different method."

"And a more tedious one." She sighed. They walked, their retinue with them, and when they entered the elevator, there were too many people to fit inside.

"We will take this one," the Director announced. The retinue held back as indicated.

When the doors closed, Sunchaser mused, "Now to see the damage."

"We are a hardy bunch, Halo. He will likely recover."

"All the more disappointing. Some things simply need to—"

"Die?" Rodheimer cut in the word harshly, his face going dark.

She looked at him, glanced at Garik, and pursed her lips in thought. "I intended to say step out of the way. No one wishes harm to Jantzen. He has been a stalwart leg of this program, indispensable. It is simply time for him to realize his usefulness is over, and we are ready to move forward without him."

"Yes," Rodheimer said, his face relaxing. "I concur. You, Halo, must also realize *how* we are moving forward."

"The boy." She didn't sound pleased.

"Of course."

"He will not take Jantzen's place. He may be in his apartment, but he does not have his—"

"I have not said he is taking Jantzen's place. We have discussed this. He is using a vacant apartment that Jantzen no longer requires. If Jantzen comes to his senses and makes this right—"

The elevator dinged, Sunchaser's expression hardened, and they moved forward before Rodheimer could finish.

Garik understood perfectly. Jantzen was being given a second chance, one that didn't make Sunchaser happy. The ribbon-floored corridor led them to a discovery that would either reveal that Jantzen had survived, or his capture had damaged him beyond repair.

At least he was alive. For that, Garik thanked God for answering his prayer.

INSIDE THE trauma ward, Garik was relieved to learn that none of those brought in with Jantzen was being dumped directly into Basement 5's holding cells for genetic misfits who hadn't matured to standard in the human-hybrid program's quest for the perfect super soldier.

The corridors bustled with people and equipment, though the melee opened into a cone of free space anywhere the Director and Sunchaser walked. Garik caught sight of Paolo, his eyes closed and his head lolling to one side, on a gurney being rolled into an operating theater. What had happened to him? There was no blood he could see, but then, with the pressure wave from the induced lightning strike . . . it had broken glass and cracked concrete. How much damage could a human body endure, even a hybrid one?

They didn't enter the operating theater where the

medical team worked on Jantzen. They viewed the goings on from a glass-fronted observation room much as Garik had been observed during his various tests and challenges. Three times during the procedure, the circlets encased Jantzen's body in a fine-meshed electric web, causing the medical team to jerk away. Each occurrence brought out the needle, and twice they patted his face, once hard, before his eyes opened and they were sure he was alive.

They were kinder, gentler than the team on the street, but still, it was hard to watch. Rodheimer was in observation mode, expressionless, but if Garik had to place an emotion on the man, it would be satisfaction. Sunchaser was more transparent. Hope flared in her with each setback, as though she hoped the man didn't survive.

The others in the room seemed to gravitate to Team Rodheimer or Team Sunchaser, picking their champion and certain they were on the winning side.

Garik was on Team Jantzen. Each time the man glitched, he whispered, "Dear God, Holy Jesus in Heaven . . ."

He needed Jantzen to live, more than anything he knew.

— 12 —

I n the days that followed, Garik worried the floor in his apartment, kicked his bedding off at night, and pounded whatever happened to be around him. Even Rodheimer kept urging him to be patient. He could visit Jantzen when he was better.

During a Devon visit, as Garik paced, Devon pointed out that he had developed a unique way of walking. Fluid, almost catlike.

"Why not?" smarted Garik. "Since I'm so unique around here, as the Director keeps telling me. A better topic, why won't they let me visit Jantzen?"

"They will. Likely today, remember, but back to my observation. Do something for me. See if you can touch the floor with your palms."

"Sheesh." Garik rolled his eyes, but he did it, bending over to place his hands flat on the floor.

"Six-four and you can do that. Okay, pretty good. How about your legs over your head?"

"This doesn't get me down to see Jantzen. Follow. My. Lead. Devo."

"No, it doesn't help get you to Jantzen, but until we get permission, that's off the table. Your legs over your head. I'm still the activities director, and I direct you to do this for me."

"Yes, Father." Garik sat, pulled his leg over his head, and look at Devon. "Good enough?"

"Does it hurt?"

"Sheesh. All the questions. How about this?" He made a pretzel of himself and walked through it before standing up, an impossible feat even circus performers would find difficult.

"I have some theories about you. I do have training in human physiology. And you are human, even if you claim you are not."

"Says the man with no extra DNA strands coursing through his blood."

"Says your friend. Hear me out."

"Yeah, yeah, Devo. Tell me all about myself. I appreciate that." Garik fell into a chair across from him and scowled.

"I've been making a list in my head—"

"About me. I'm glad you think about me so much."

"Take it down a notch, kiddo. I feel like I'm your friend, but I'm also over your health and welfare, even if you do live in the clouds now. So, one. We know you're taller. The way you just moved tells me your spine has developed a level of flexibility only seen in cheetahs, some of the fastest animals on the planet."

"Timber wolf. Let's keep to the correct species."

"I'm just giving my observations. Two, your tendons, they have become more elastic, as proven by the pretzel boy."

"Tsh!" Garik was paying attention now. "What else?"

"That enormous chest? Not all muscle. I guarantee that if we ran you though an MRI machine, we'd confirm larger lungs with greater air capacity and a massive heart that pumps two or three times the blood volume as us normal folk. Mind you, I would like some of that, so that isn't a criticism."

"And my headaches?" He had shared the throbbing resonance, just not the rainbows. No one, and that meant no one could know about those.

"I think that has to do with your sense of smell."

"Yeah, right, Devo." Garik laughed. "How does my sense of smell have anything to do with my head?"

"First, your nose is in your head. Second, something in there has to make room to smell all those smells. I don't know about the size of the canine nasal cavity, but there's forty times more olfactory receptors in a dog's nasal cavity than in mine. And I bet there's a forty times greater spot in the brain to process all that information. Your brain is making room for that."

"And giving me headaches in the process."

"And likely using up all the space your common sense used to use. Now, when we get you back to the basement where all the interesting people live, how about we test those new tendons and that flexible spine on the climbing wall? I think it's time to get a new name on the leaderboard."

Garik cocked his head, absorbing the question.

"And that, too. Have you noticed how you tilt your head when you decide you're interested in what you're hearing? Don't give everything away. Hasn't anyone ever told you that?"

And that brought them back to Jantzen, the man who had taught him that lesson. He had to find out how he was doing, and he was through being told no. He stood.

"Now, Devo. Your passkey will take us down there. We have to check on Jantzen."

"Whoa-ho." Devon tapped the cast he had worn for

nearly two months. "Just let me remind you that this is your fault. What else do you want me to give up for you? My arm next time? My neck?"

"That cast is about to come off. This is just an elevator ride, and the Director made it clear that Sunchaser has no say on my training in the basement or elsewhere. Say I got hurt on the climbing wall. My carabiner broke and I fell. Everyone knows I'm abysmal at climbing."

"And I know you heal like that." Devon snapped his fingers. "Something else I'd like to have. Okay, what's there to lose? Just my job. Help me to my feet."

Garik took his hand and pulled him erect, only to have Devon lean into him and intentionally catch his ankle with his good foot. Garik, overbalanced, let go of the man and hit the floor hard.

"There, first payment on whatever happens to me because I'm doing this for you. Surprised you didn't see that coming. Now, let's go."

Garik was surprised, too, and attributed it to trust. He'd had no reason to suspect Devon was about to force him down. He grinned, found his feet, and handed the man his crutches.

Jantzen would be fine. He was the best at everything. Nothing could beat the man down. Nothing.

THEY EXPECTED the elevator to carry them all the way to Basement Level 4 where the hospital was located. It stopped on the research center's lobby level on Basement 1. Security were at the door, and they instructed them to exit the car.

"No cars to the lower levels," they said, "and no traffic up. We will let you know when access is reinstated."

"We're stuck here?" Devon asked.

"I'm afraid so, sir. You can help yourself to lobby seating or visit the cafeteria." He pointed to the tables through a wide doorway just past the lobby.

"Sure." Devon glanced at the distance they needed to travel and hefted his crutches. "A wheelchair or a scooter would be nice."

"Certainly. Right here, sir." The man pulled a manual wheelchair from behind a column. He took the crutches, handed them to Garik, and adjusted a support to hold up Devon's cast.

"Thank you." Garik nodded, took pilot's position, and maneuvered Devon towards the cafeteria. Devon sent Garik for a snack, and he returned with a tray of gooey breakfast sweets.

"What's this?" Devon touched one, licked his finger, and nodded approvingly. "Never mind. Good choice."

"Not a choice. It's all they had. Have you noticed the school of fish swimming upstream?" He motioned to just outside the cafeteria. A steady flow of people, some hybridized, even more not, swelled the direction of the underground parking garage. Many looked to be from the center's office staff housed on Level 1, with others garbed in military drab. Voices leaked into Garik's ears.

"She actually has it out."

"I never thought it was real."

"Do you think she'll use it? Wouldn't that be a story to tell."

A hybrid—boasting imposing red eyes and the leathery skin of a crocodile—exposed large, pointed teeth as he called excitedly to a companion, "Someone's breaking Jantzen out!" They were pushing others out of their way as they ran.

Click, click. The gears in Garik's head turned. Information in, compute the values, extrapolate an outcome. *She* could only be Sunchaser. *It* . . . the sword. The one time he had seen it in action, she had used it to eliminate a dissenting opponent. The final value was *Jantzen*. With the circlets on Jantzen's wrists and legs, it wouldn't be a fair fight.

"Now, Devon." He stood. "It's time to move. Whatever's going on involves Sunchaser's electrified sword and Jantzen."

"And you know this how?" Devon crammed the last of a sweet bun into his mouth.

"I cocked my head. Now, or I'm leaving you here."

THROUGH THE doors to the parking garage, even

with his height, the crush of people blocked Garik's view. The military drab had fists raised and hooted for their choice of champions. Despite the riot-charged atmosphere, Brace's paramilitary, lodged at the high school, had yet to arrive.

The crocodile man yelled, "She has it charged, and the Director's not even around."

Sunchaser. Why would she have the sword out now? A flying creature with long limbs, thick in the forearms, and legs that bent in an unusual way caught his attention. Massive eyes and a pointed snout told of its insect DNA, and wings at its back thrummed the air. Justin Kurtew! The man had . . . continued to evolve in the time since Garik had seen him. Now, Garik was having a hard time finding the man in the mantis hybrid.

"Devon, stay here." Garik leaped on a concrete barrier for a better view. Beyond the press of the onlookers and their cheers and chants, Halo Sunchaser vibrated with intent in an all-black kaftan with a thick cloth belt in deep red. Her headwrap matched her belt, and with her ebony skin, she was frightening. The electrified sword glittered in her hand, spitting white sparks that kissed the ground with black-painted stars.

Justin hovered over a disoriented and stumbling Jantzen Hefferly. The circlets at his arms and ankles flashed, electricity formed a spiderweb over his body, and he staggered.

Garik looked to an opening in the crowd and found Alyna Lindberg, modified with a Komodo dragon. Her claws of glasslike keratin were more razor blade than bony material, and if she were the one rescuing Jantzen, the reinforced doors in the basements were no match for her. Garik expected she had left some badly damaged infrastructure in her wake for Jantzen to reach this far.

Metal echoed against metal, a door slamming back, and an earthquake of a voice rumbled.

"Halo, you cannot continue to use the sword this way. It is inappropriate and unacceptable." The mass of people parted as Weston Rodheimer strode her way, an angry storm threatening to lash out in roiling waves of destruction.

Cannot continue. The words jumped at Garik. Rodheimer and Sunchaser had worked together when he had last seen the sword in action. *What else had she done with it?*

"Leave it, Weston. I will end this once and for all." Sunchaser tracked Jantzen, Alyna, and Justin. The sword backed up her words with jagged fingers of crackling lightning.

"You have an audience. Have you noticed?"

"And that means?" Her eyes shifted and locked on Jantzen with hawklike intensity. His circlets flashed, and he stumbled once again. Alyna stepped to him to help him.

"He means nothing to you, Halo," Alyna yelled.

"He means everything to me. Step back, Alyna. You and the flying creature can go free. Jantzen is mine."

Halo grasped the hilt in both hands and lifted it over her head, pointing it toward the ceiling. Energy leaped from the tip and splayed across the concrete overhead, and when she let it fall, the full force of its charge surged to envelop Jantzen. Throughout the underground facility, lighting fixtures on the ceiling brightened and shattered as the sword's power coursed through the air.

"No!" Garik yelled, and he unleashed the rainbows swirling in his head. They were his arrows, his lightning bolts, his coin to ride Charon's boat to the other side and back again to retrieve what mustn't be lost. The people around him flashed with brilliantly colored swirls, the ceiling swam with red and blue and purple, and even Justin became a rainbow bridge, a Bifröst arc leaping through the air to grant access to Asgard, the fabled city of the Norse gods. Ragnarök hovered at the edges of Garik's perception in distant echoes of impending cacophony.

Even so, there were a hundred people in Garik's way. He couldn't go through them. He had to go around each one, and electricity can travel faster than even the quickest hybrid, even when melded with the DNA of a timber wolf and given tendons of steel, bellows for lungs, and a heart that could pump an ocean of blood.

He did get to watch the circlets around Jantzen's wrists and ankles tumble to the floor of the garage as Jantzen was eaten by the power of the sword. With Jantzen gone, Garik's rainbows fled, leaving him a dozen feet short of Sunchaser. He collapsed to his knees, exhausted with the energy he had expended. Alyna let out a shriek of frustration, and she turned and began to run. Justin, freak that he was, dipped, adjusted his attitude, and flashed after her.

Sunchaser raised the sword in victory. Many in the crowd—too many—cheered with her.

Rodheimer exploded in anger, electrical sparks of his own burning those who stood too close.

Garik was overcome with dismay, and his anger surged through him. Sunchaser! How could she? He had watched part of himself die as Jantzen was eaten by the sword.

He remembered a quote his priest once shared: Vengeance is mine, sayeth the Lord!

And mine, decided Garik. As soon as I figure out how.

In Book Nine, Garik Shayk learns that truth is not always as it seems.

The Electrified Sword
Book Nine
The Human-Hybrid Project

Garik Shayk is stunned when Halo Sunchaser is celebrated for killing Garik's mentor and closest ally. He comes to believe Sunchaser authored his girlfriend's death. He is certain that if he learns the secret to the electrified sword and the people it kills, he can bring Sunchaser to her knees. It might be too late for Marisa, but no one else has to die!

The Human-Hybrid Project

Addictive!

A 10-book series you won't be able to forget. Explore each book, the characters, and more at our website www.thehumanhybridproject.com.

Book 1   Book 2

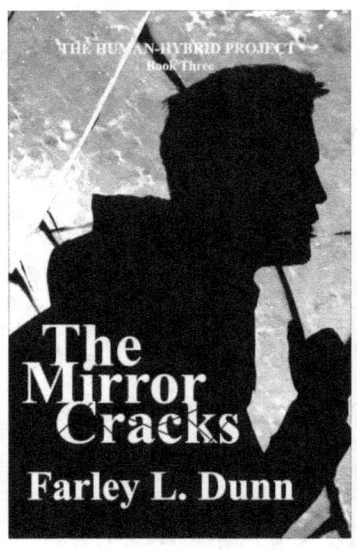

Book 3

Book 4

Book 5

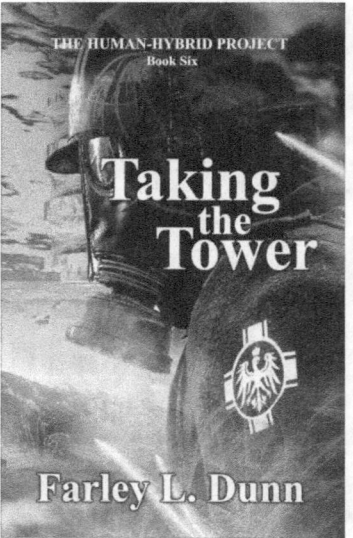

Book 6

Book 7

Book 8

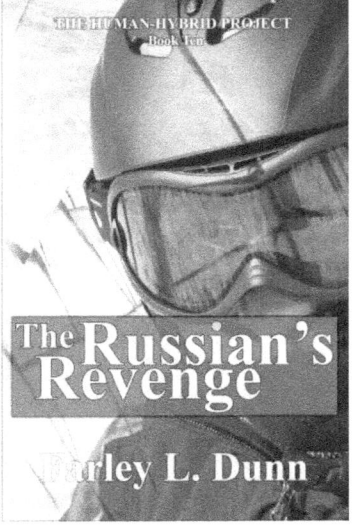

Book 9

Book 10

www.ingramcontent.com/pod-product-compliance
Lightning Source LLC
Chambersburg PA
CBHW070558180626
46817CB00005B/1902